SPY CAT
SAFARI

ANDREW COPE
Ably and significantly assisted by Will Hussey

Illustrated by James de la Rue

PUFFIN

PUFFIN BOOKS

UK | USA | Canada | Ireland | Australia
India | New Zealand | South Africa

Puffin Books is part of the Penguin Random House group of companies
whose addresses can be found at global.penguinrandomhouse.com.

puffinbooks.com

Penguin
Random House
UK

First published 2015
001

Text copyright © Andrew Cope, 2015
Illustrations copyright © James de la Rue, 2015

The moral right of the author and illustrator has been asserted

Set in 15/18 pt Bembo Book MT Std
Typeset by Jouve (UK), Milton Keynes
Printed in Great Britain by Clays Ltd, St Ives plc

A CIP catalogue record for this book is available from the British Library

ISBN: 978–0–141–35718–8

www.greenpenguin.co.uk

*For George Edmund Cook. 'Eddie'. Who put
the 'great' into 'great-granddad'*

1. Preying Pray

The New Forest, Hampshire, England

The professor waded through the river to try and lose them but he could still hear the dogs. He paused for a moment, listening intently. He imagined them, tails raised, noses to the ground, slobbering in pursuit. They were getting closer. He ran for the safety of the trees, his feet squelching. He was trying to stay low in case the enemy was close. The professor wasn't cut out for this. He was the wrong side of middle age and his liking for late-night snacks meant his midriff was rounder than it should be. He trained spy animals but wasn't spy material himself. Yet here he was, being hunted.

He slumped at the base of the tree, chest heaving. The lens in the left eye of his spectacles was shattered, the frame bent. Sweat seeped from his eyebrows, blurring his vision even more. He tugged the lab coat from his shoulders.

'It's making me an easy target,' he cursed, noticing that it was now more red than white. The professor winced, wondering how many times he'd been hit. He pressed his hand against his upper arm. *Red*. 'These enemy agents are good,' he grimaced, suspecting the end was near.

Professor Cortex peered round the tree, squinting into the forest. He covered his left eye to help him focus. He remembered the map and was fairly sure that if he could just get through the clearing, there was a cabin.

Maybe it's got Wi-Fi or a phone, he thought. *It's my only chance*.

His thinking was dulled by a sudden pain in his chest. He rummaged for his pillbox, opened it and scoffed a handful. He coughed as the pills got stuck in his dry throat.

The enemy agent pricked his ears. A cough was enough. He settled into position, eye pressed

to the sight of the gun. He was hidden halfway up a tree.

Perfect for a sniper, he breathed. He scanned the clearing. He'd hit him once and knew the old man was struggling. *Chances are he'll be making for the cabin. I can wait*, he thought, scanning again through the sights of the rifle. The cross picked out a white lab coat and his body stiffened. 'Bingo!'

The professor swallowed hard, three times, and the pills finally disappeared. The barking was getting louder. He liked dogs, but not *these* dogs! He took one last squint into the clearing and went for it. He'd seen Spy Dog run from baddies and he knew that he had a better chance if he zigzagged. For some reason, he couldn't help yelling.

The agent in the tree relaxed. He'd been taught by the best. The old man was doing the slowest zigzagging run in history. *And all that noise? Tut tut – big mistake, old man.*

The sniper eased the trigger and Professor Cortex fell, clutching his leg. The assassin smiled. *Down but not quite out. This is fun!* The

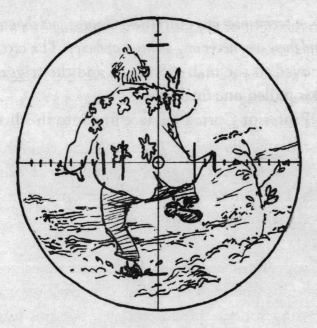

man was up again, staggering across the clearing, red footprints in the dirt. The second shot caught him on the shoulder and he reeled in agony.

'No more!' he yelled. 'Please. Enough!' He was on his knees, hands held high, shouting into the trees. 'See? No weapon. I'm unarmed. Have mercy.'

The hunter licked his lips, his eyes unblinking. His mission was clear. Eliminate the professor.

I can't remember any instructions about second chances and there was never any mention of mercy. The cross moved to the man's forehead and the trigger was pulled one final time.

Professor Cortex fell face first into the dirt.

2. Panda-monium

Edinburgh Zoo, Scotland — the same day

Pandas aren't known for their speed, so catching them wasn't the problem. Lifting them out of their enclosure was going to be the tricky part. And as Gus had already noted, 'Without anyone noticing? Almost impossible!'

Everyone knows that owners look like their dogs. If zoo-goers looked like animals then Gus was a silverback gorilla, his nose broken so many times that their profiles matched exactly. His shoulders were almost double the width of his waist, and his hands were like clubs. Tattoos oozed brazenly out of each shirtsleeve, trouser leg and a few other places besides.

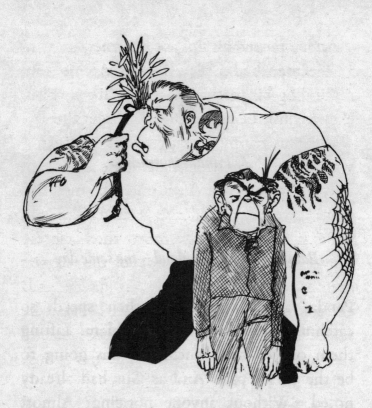

Archie was also a primate lookalike. He was small-framed and hairy with slumped shoulders and low-hanging knuckles. Tufts of black hair peeped out of the top of his shirt and his eyes darted nervously from beneath one long eyebrow.

'It's a good job you don't have a big red bottom,' joked Gus, 'otherwise they'd keep you in a cage.'

Archie pursed his lips and frowned.

The men had a plan. Or, as Archie kept reminding his partner in crime, 'It's *my* plan. You are just the muscle. Don't forget that.'

Gus was happy to play to his strength – which was . . . his strength. If these pandas got ugly, he would sort them out. The men had spent a lovely day wandering around Edinburgh Zoo. If anyone had watched them closely they'd have noticed that most of the day was spent loitering and observing outside the panda enclosure. But nobody did notice because the majority of visitors were doing exactly the same. As the tour guide kept explaining, 'These are the only two pandas in the whole of the British Isles.'

Archie checked his watch. He wanted to be sure that he and Gus were hiding in the reptile house at closing time. It was dark and warm and Archie had been right – nobody disturbed them. By 10 p.m. the zoo was locked and all the staff had gone home. The men emerged at midnight when everything was quiet except for the occasional squealing and howling of a few nocturnal residents. Gus's teeth chattered – a mixture of cold, excitement and fear. He kept reminding Archie that these weren't ordinary pandas.

'They're called *giant* pandas!'

And Archie kept reminding Gus that he wasn't a normal human being, he was a *giant* human being. And that was why he was there.

The shady pair spent an hour assembling their pulley. Archie looked satisfied as they finally manoeuvred it right up to the glass wall of the panda enclosure.

'In you go, big man,' urged Archie.

'But . . .' began his partner, losing his nerve. 'What if the pandas get angry?' It didn't seem quite so black and white any more.

'Stop being such a wuss,' hissed Archie. 'These pandas aren't angry . . . they're *hungry*. And you've got a sack of their favouritest snack.'

Gus patted the bag. 'Bamboo,' he reminded himself. 'They eat bamboo, right? Not people.'

Archie rolled his eyes in the darkness. He slapped Gus as he ushered him into the cage. 'They never eat people,' he said as he slid the bolt into place. 'Well, *hardly* ever.'

Gus rattled the cage door nervously. A small squeak of wind escaped from his bottom.

'Right, I'm lifting you in,' said Archie, cranking the handle of what looked like a giant fishing rod with a cage suspended on the end. Gus whimpered a little as the cage was elevated. When he was higher than the glass wall Archie swung the contraption until Gus was hovering on the other side of the panda enclosure.

'Now doooown you go,' said Archie, turning the handle the other way. There was a larger blast of nervous gas from Gus's bottom as the cage landed softly on the grass, on the pandas' side of the enclosure.

Gus's flashlight shone around. 'Tian Tian,' he whispered hesitantly. 'Yang Guang. I have a midnight snack for you.' Gus opened his bag and held a branch of bamboo out in front of him. 'Snackeroony. Bamberoony. Come and get it.'

The pandas were grumpy. They'd been up all day entertaining the crowds and now their sleep was being rudely interrupted. The male panda, Yang Guang, wandered out to see what all the noise was about. His eyesight wasn't great but his sense of smell told him there was some bamboo to be had. He beckoned to his mate and they lumbered towards Gus, their white patches looming out of the darkness.

Gus gulped and stepped backwards. He was a big and wild man but pandas were even bigger and considerably wilder. There was another high-pitched squeak of gas as he nervously enticed the bears towards the cage and tossed the bag inside. The pandas first sniffed Gus and then the cage. Their decision was easy. The sleepy bears climbed into the cage and started chomping.

Gus quickly shut the door and fumbled the bolt into place. 'Go, go, go!' he whisper-shouted, trying to keep his excitement under wraps.

Archie did the rest, reeling in the giant catch, the pandas landing on the freedom side of the

enclosure. He was sorely tempted to leave Gus inside the zoo as he looked quite at home there. Gus thought otherwise, however, and wandered back through the side door before bolting it behind him. The bears were collared and silently led away, happily munching, through the main entrance and out into the car park. Once inside the van, Archie looked over at his big-boned and small-brained accomplice and shook his head once more.

Next day's security footage showed white patches in procession, headlights flickering on and a van leaving the car park. Darkness had been the criminals' only weapon. One of the newspapers gleefully reported that it had been 'Panda-monium at Edinburgh Zoo'.

3. Professor Caught-X

Meanwhile, back in the New Forest, Spy Dog and the pups had given up searching for Professor Cortex. They were making a hot chocolate in the cabin when there was scratching at the door. Lara put her paw to her mouth to signify 'shush'. She grabbed her weapon, stood on her hind legs and peered out of the window. She beckoned to Spud and Star to open the door.

'Quickly, guys. It's him!'

Star was the smallest and therefore the lightest of the puppies. She knew the routine. Her brother squatted and she climbed on to his shoulders. Spud took a deep breath and eased himself to his feet, holding his sister high enough to reach the door handle. Star pulled the handle and the door swung open.

Professor Cortex fell into the cabin. His breathing was shallow and rattling. His spectacles were gone, smashed by the same bullet that had smeared his face in red.

'I need help,' he gasped.

'Quickly, pups, get him in and lie him down on the sofa. He's in a bad way. Help me find his tablets.'

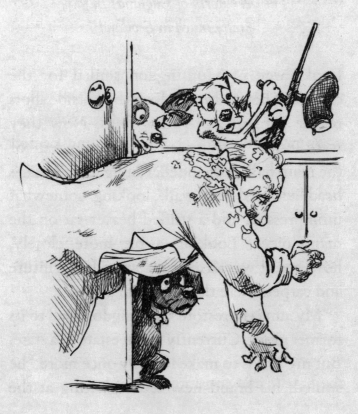

4. Huntingdon Hall

*The very north of England. In fact,
pretty much in Scotland*

Lord Large of Huntingdon smiled for the camera. They'd already done the outside shots of the gardens and rolling hills. Now they were inside, surrounded by the grandeur of the main hall. A chandelier hung low. A stag's head adorned the wall, looking somewhat unimpressed, and a stuffed beaver sat on the mantelpiece. Looking a bit more closely, however, it was all a bit shabby. The furniture and carpets were threadbare in places.

'My aim is to restore Huntingdon Hall to its former glory. Currently it's an estate in a state. But my aim is to make it *stately* once more,' he smiled, his brand-new teeth glinting at the

reporter from the *Berwick Chronicle*. 'At the moment the roof leaks, the gardens are wild and the bedrooms are damp. It's heartbreaking that a house of such historical importance has been allowed to become so run down.'

The reporter was scribbling furiously. 'So what are your plans, Your Lordship?'

'I'm very interested in local history. As you are probably aware, this old house was at one time used as a game reserve. My wonderful staff and I will be returning it to its former glory. A century ago, this estate was famous for deer stalking and grouse shooting. My goal is for it to be a thriving hunting ground once more. My plan is to put the *hunt* back into Huntingdon Hall.'

No sooner had the reporter disappeared to file his story about the new owner of Huntingdon Hall, than the work began. Heavy lorries arrived and yellow diggers tore up the land. Within a month the 500-acre estate was circled by a six-metre-high electric fence. Just to be sure, a line of razor wire sat atop, alongside dozens of signs that shouted *DANGER OF DEATH*. Outside the fence was a sheer three-metre-deep moat full of swampy water. There was only one way in – an imposing iron gate, guarded by two burly men. Cameras dotted the estate so Lord Large could keep an eye on proceedings.

After all the work was completed the lord of the manor declared himself satisfied. 'Nobody gets in and nobody gets out. Not without me knowing.' He thrust a lever in his office and the electric fence buzzed into life.

5. Bottom Secret

The professor's lab. Location CLASSIFIED

No matter how often they'd visited, none of the children were particularly comfortable with this part. The entrance to the professor's top-secret laboratory was always well hidden and this time it seemed especially well disguised. And after his recent scare in the New Forest, the children were concerned that the old Professor Cortex would be back, fit and well again.

Ben looked at the printed sheet and shrugged. 'This is it,' he said, beckoning to the small blue Portaloo.

'Maybe it's like a TARDIS,' beamed Ollie. 'Massive on the inside.'

One by one, taking care not to be seen, each of them had sidled into the small blue cubicle. There they all stood, somewhat squashed, huddled round the beckoning toilet.

'It might be where Dr Who does a poo,' suggested Ollie.

Sophie and Ollie both looked towards Ben, who let out another shrug.

'Three flushes,' he said, tapping the instructions. The boy's hand reached for the handle and the toilet flushed, dark blue water gushing down the hole. All eyes went back to Ben. He pulled the handle and got that empty sound when the toilet hasn't yet refilled. 'And one for luck,' he said, yanking the handle a third time.

There was a humming sound as the floor started to descend. A minute later the toilet cubicle came to a halt and Sophie reached for the door handle. The children stepped out into the professor's secret underground laboratory where a young man was waiting. He ushered them along several brilliant-white corridors to a door marked *Inventing Room*. The children looked at each other but no one said anything. They all hoped that Professor Cortex hadn't been replaced – or worse . . .

For his part, the scientist had spent an hour in the bath, soothing his aching limbs and wiping the paint off his body. He stood, ruddy-faced, wearing a crisp new lab coat, replacement spectacles and a very wide grin. The only evidence of the paintballing was a swollen left eye. The professor tapped the new bottle of indigestion tablets in his lab coat. He let out a small burp.

'Pardon me,' he beamed, as the children came into view.

The children were relieved to see the professor's smiling head, and the three wagging tails.

It was only the cat that looked downbeat. Shakespeare sensed he'd played his part well in the training exercise – maybe a bit too well. Professor Cortex was evidently more suited to operating behind the scenes and had become a little flustered.

The cat stood up and stretched his paws. *When humans say try your best they don't always mean it.* Shakespeare sighed. He still had a lot to learn about being a spy cat.

'Come on in, kiddie-winks,' smiled the scientist. 'And no need to feel bad, Agent Cat. You were excellent. In fact,' he coughed, 'puuurfect. You outperformed the dogs in the paintballing exercise.'

It was the cat's turn to look bright and the dogs' to sag. The pups had been teasing the new recruit about dogs being better than cats so it was nice to score a victory. Shakespeare's

mission had been clear. He recalled the conversation from this morning. 'I'm a great believer in making things as real as possible,' the professor had said. 'You can learn about weapons from reading books but the best way is to get hands-on, or, *ahem*, "paws-on" experience.' And that was that. The professor and the spy-pet team had arrived at the paintballing centre and each animal had been issued with a weapon. It had been difficult at first with paws instead of fingers but the professor wasn't one for excuses. 'Deal with it,' he'd said dismissively with a wave of the hand. 'I'm the hunted. You give me twenty minutes' head start and then you come after me. We meet back in the cabin – here,' he said, jabbing his finger somewhere on the map, 'in two hours. And the winner will be the one who shoots me the most times.'

GM451 was a product of the professor's elite spy-dog training school. She was the original Licensed Assault and Rescue Animal, affectionately named Lara, the world's first ever qualified spy dog. She'd captured more baddies and been on more missions than Shakespeare had had catnaps at the Cooks' house. Lara was issued with blue paint bullets. She fully intended to *blue* away the competition.

Spud, with yellow bullets, was second favourite. He was proud to be a spy pup with three successful missions under his belt. And, speaking of belts, he was the pup who needed one the most. Spud called it 'puppy fat' but everyone else knew it was just a weakness for Ben & Jerry's. Spud was an expert gamer and was hoping to put his Xbox skills to good use in what he was calling 'Mission Paintball'.

Star, his sister, was a sleek, black and white running machine. For this activity she was third favourite simply because she wasn't as strong as her brother, her rifle weighing heavily with purple paint pellets. What Star lacked in strength she made up for in determination. She was an astute and quietly confident spy pup.

Shakespeare was the newest addition to the spy pets' team, with a raggedy ear as evidence that he'd already been involved in a couple of missions. He was proud to represent the cat species. He was mostly ginger with white paws and a white underbelly. Shakespeare's gleaming green eyes gave him the advantage of night-time vision, and his sharp claws allowed him to climb trees. So, although not as loud or aggressive as the dogs, he considered himself to be a ginger ninja, a superhero of the feline kind.

He knew he had a lot of catching up to do and had lately done away with catnaps, investing his time in surfing the internet and watching James Bond movies. Best of all,

Professor Cortex had issued Shakespeare with a translating collar. He wore it proudly, its small red flashing light translating human language into cat language. As a result, he loved reading, and was halfway through the Harry Potter series. He'd checked his red paint bullets and slung the heavy rifle round his back. Nobody was expecting the cat to win. *Mission Im-puss-i-ball* was what they'd said.

He'd shrugged. *The pressure's off. I have nothing to lose.*

Shakespeare swished his tail as he reflected on this morning's paintballing adventure. *I used my brain. Dogs have a better sense of smell, right? So, they stuck their noses to the ground and off they went. I knew the old man had twenty minutes' head start but also that he wouldn't have got very far. Sure enough, he'd craftily crossed a river to throw off the scent. And that's when my tree climbing came into its own.*

Shakespeare had peeled off from the dogs and used his feline advantage to climb the highest tree. The wannabe spy cat ran through the day's events in his mind, wondering if his performance was up to scratch.

In the distance was a white-coated runner. I easily managed to get a couple of shots in so his coat was splattered with red — just so the dogs would know. As the old man came nearer he looked like he'd overdone it. But, hey, orders are orders. This was not a mercy mission. I was instructed to hunt the professor. Cat versus dogs. So that final head shot was justified. I pulled the trigger and bang . . .

When he'd enquired about the other rules he was told very bluntly that there was only one that mattered: *the safety of the children . . .*

Hence the cat was a little uncomfortable that Sophie's mobile phone had a screensaver of her precious mog in a full-action pose.

It's hardly blending into the background, he thought, whenever he watched Sophie scroll through the pictures with her school pals.

Sophie was so proud of Shakespeare. *Her cat!* 'You actually outperformed the dogs!' she clapped. She knew, and Shakespeare knew, that although he was officially the family's pet, he really belonged to the little girl. His favourite place was a warm indentation in Sophie's duvet and there was nothing he loved more than a lazy morning on Sophie's lap while the little girl busied herself with drawing and painting.

Sophie loved Lara and the pups but there was something special about the cat/girl bond. And this was even stronger since the cat actually saved Sophie's life during a daring rescue in London. 'My hero!' she kept saying as she swept her hand across his ginger back.

For his part Shakespeare was proud to be part of the spy pets' team. He couldn't help purring every time Sophie called him a 'hero' or a 'ginger ninja'. He had worked hard, putting in hours of extra learning in his own time to make sure he was up to scratch. While the family slept he'd prowled the streets, his special translating collar enabling him to read and understand. He'd tried to expand his comfort zone and do what the professor had said was 'beyond an ordinary cat', so he'd learnt to skateboard. He was handy with a barbecue, and he knew a thing or two about first aid.

And while he had settled into life as the family's puss, he understood that this was no ordinary family. Lara and the pups were no ordinary pets. He was part of a super-elite team of special agents, ready to be called into action at any time.

The professor's instructions were still ringing in his ears: *Act normal. Blend in. Draw no attention to yourself. And never forget the golden rule: the safety of the children is your number-one priority.*

The furry assassin was brought back to the here and now by the professor's voice, his collar flashing in unison. 'And now I've washed all that yucky red paint off, how about I reveal some of my latest inventions?'

6. Gone Walkies

You didn't need to be a catwalk expert to know that the professor knew nothing at all about fashion. To him, clothes were more about keeping warm than staying cool.

'I'm not sure about the baseball cap, Prof,' winced Sophie, voicing everyone's thoughts aloud. 'You're the world's most amazing scientist and everything. So, white coat? Yes. Spectacles? Absolutely. Sandals and socks. Just about OK . . . for you, that is. But baseball cap? Probably not. And sideways? A definite no-no . . .'

'It's absolutely not a *baseball* cap!' snapped the professor. 'It's my latest invention. It's a *thinking* cap.'

'Well, we're thinking that you might be too old to wear it,' chuckled Ben. 'You look like you're auditioning to be in the oldest boy band in the world. The Pensioners, perhaps?'

'Or maybe The Nerds?' suggested Ollie.

The professor pushed his spectacles back up to the bridge of his nose. He burped and looked flustered. 'I'm not a pensioner and I'm not a nerd. I'm a geek,' said the old man proudly. 'And my hat is not a fashion statement,' he added, although he twisted the cap round all the same. 'It's a science statement. This,' he said, pointing to his headwear, 'is possibly my best ever invention. GM451, please flick on the TV. Channel 1001.'

Lara hit the remote and a black screen crackled into life. After a couple of seconds large white words appeared on channel 1001.

'Blast and damnation. Now, where are my pills?' The professor flapped at his pockets.

'Your pills are on the table,' said Sophie.

The professor stared at the little girl for a moment; his lips were sealed, but words were mysteriously appearing on the TV. 'Well, for heaven's sake, get them for me before I pass out completely! Young people nowadays. Always so critical. No common sense whatsoever!'

The professor looked at the screen and removed his hat. 'Erm . . . sorry about that,' he said. 'I didn't really mean you to see those words. But it would be nice if you marvelled at my inventions instead of rubbishing them.'

Lara and the pups were wagging hard.

'Ma,' woofed Star, 'is that what I think it is?'

'My, ahem, *thinking cap*,' said the professor, raising an eyebrow in the hope that the group might marvel at the clever name, 'is a thought translator.' He placed it on Ollie's head and continued. 'Everyone's head is full of thoughts. In fact, you cannot *not* think,' he beamed. 'The hat contains a chip that absorbs those thoughts – well, a mixture of brain impulses and emotions actually. The trick is to make sure you capture the product of both the ganglia and amygdala. The hat causes the dendrites and synapses to fuse, creating a pulse of . . .'

Ollie yawned and fidgeted from one foot to the other. The words *I'm bored* appeared on the screen, followed by *What on earth is the old bloke on about?* and *I need a wee*.

The professor looked at the screen and paused. 'I see. Yes, well, basically, the hat

translates thoughts into words. So whatever the wearer is thinking is revealed on the screen.'

Ollie took off the hat and dashed to the toilet.

Spud's whole body was wagging. 'Does it work on dogs?' he yapped, snatching the hat and donning it backwards in what he was hoping might be a cool-dog look.

All eyes went to the TV screen where Spud answered his own question. The words *doughnut*, *fries* and *milkshake* revealed that the puppy really did have a one-track mind.

'Snack time soon, Agent Pup,' promised the scientist, snatching the cap off Spud and pulling it on to his own bald scalp. The pup's tail immediately stopped wagging. Evidently the fast food was not coming fast enough.

'Anything else, Prof?' asked Ben excitedly.

'Well,' he sighed, 'I have this rather thrilling work in progress.' He marched into a walk-in cupboard and emerged with a small aeroplane. 'It's a model of one of those old Wright brothers' biplanes,' he said. 'Remote control. And it flies,' he said. 'Obviously.'

'A small remote-control plane is pretty cool,' agreed Ben. 'But I think you'll find that it's already been invented.'

The TV screen broke out in a series of complicated equations as the professor's head began to warm up. 'Not only does this one have a spy camera, so it can be used to fly into tricky situations and gather data –'

'Except the baddies would hear it,' interrupted Sophie, rolling her eyes.

'And that's where you're utterly wrong,' snapped the scientist. 'This is a silent spy plane. I've invented a *silent* engine.' The TV screen was exploding with numbers and letters forming complicated computations. 'Traditional engines require fuel that is then internally combusted to produce forward thrust . . .'

The TV screen was ablaze with formulae and although the children's eyes had glazed over, the professor continued. 'Whereas this uses air. Fresh and freely available air! The small engine, here, is used to get the spy plane moving on the runway, but once it reaches optimum speed the engine cuts out and my special *airo-engine* –' he looked up momentarily, but nobody was marvelling – 'filters fresh air through these slits, where it is compressed to such a high pressure that it powers the propellers.'

He paused, eyebrows raised as the TV continued to pour out a stream of higgledy-piggledy numbers and letters in highbrow calculations.

'A totally silent plane,' Sophie marvelled, understanding the basic gist of what the professor had said (or thought).

'As I said, a work in progress,' beamed the scientist. 'This one is being tested. The early signs are very promising. And then we simply apply the technology to passenger jets. And

trains and cars. Totally silent travel,' he smiled, hopping on the spot in what Sophie called the mad-professor dance. 'And, of course, no petrol or diesel required. So totally green too. I mean, one doesn't want to blow one's own trumpet or anything, but I think I might have saved the planet!' The words *Sir Maximus*

Cortex, OBE. Services to science, saviour of the universe appeared on the screen until the professor sheepishly removed his thinking cap and muttered an apology.

Picking up the remote, he flicked to his favourite channel, BBC News 24. The TV was on silent, subtitles appearing below the news story of the day. Lara noticed it was about a dog. She motioned to the professor to turn up the volume. All eyes went to the TV, a worried news reporter looking earnestly into the camera. There were dogs everywhere.

'And how did the thief get away with such a valuable animal?' asked the lady in the studio.

The reporter put her hand to her ear to make sure she got the question. 'There's a terrific noise here at Crufts,' she said. 'As you know, this is the biggest dog show in the world. This year's winner is a very rare Japanese Akita who, to the untrained eye, looks rather like a wolf and whose pedigree name is –' she paused to look down at her notes – '*Alfonzo Haruko Wasabi Fujomaki III*. And it seems Alfonzo has simply disappeared. Gone walkies,' she said, evidently pleased to have sneaked that phrase into a dognapping story.

'Yes,' said the TV anchor, 'but how exactly can the rarest dog in the world just . . . *disappear*?'

'That, Miranda, is a very good question. And at this moment in time, nobody at Crufts is able to provide us with an answer. All I can say is that the police are investigating and everyone at this most famous of dog shows is in total shock. This is the first ever dog theft from this prestigious puppy parade. A big reward has been offered to anyone who can find Alfonzo. Back to the studio.'

'A big reward?' wagged Spud, suddenly taking a keen interest. 'Maybe that's a lasagne, or something?'

Lara gave her son a disapproving glance. 'Can you switch your one-track mind on to being a spy dog instead of a pie dog?' she woofed.

The professor was looking worried. 'That,' he huffed, 'is the final straw. I will not stand by and see these animals being kidnapped. Pet-pinched? Animal-ambushed? Whatever.'

'What animals?' asked Ollie, returning from the toilet.

The scientist strode over to the wall where he'd pinned a series of pictures and newspaper clippings. Ben, Sophie, Ollie and the spy animals gathered round, Shakespeare sitting on a table, swishing his tail and concentrating hard. 'I've been tracking the news,' said the professor. 'I've worked with animals all my life.' He looked at Lara. Nobody saw the words scrolling on the TV screen on the other side of the room. *I love you, GM451. You are my most amazing invention. I am so proud* . . . He swiped the thinking cap from his head and took a deep breath. 'I love all animals. But I'm especially interested in *special* animals. Like these,' he said, sweeping his hand across the board. 'Top left is Red Drum, the Grand National winner. Disappeared into thin air three weeks ago. Horse-napped. Stolen. In broad daylight. Imagine . . . the nerve of these people!'

'And the pandas?' asked Sophie, pointing at the next picture. 'I saw that story on the news. They were kidnapped from a zoo in Scotland.'

'Panda-napped,' corrected the professor. 'In broad moonlight. But what you probably won't have missed is this.' He jabbed a finger at a picture of an elephant.

'Cooool. How do you steal an elephant?' marvelled Ollie, thinking there must be a joke there somewhere.

'Spirited away from Whipsnade. As was this furry creature,' continued the professor, looking serious and jabbing a finger at the

tarantula at the bottom right of the board. 'Spider-snatched. An elaborate web of deceit.'

Sophie shivered.

'Exactly!' nodded the prof. 'Obviously, the government is trying to keep these thefts hush-hush. If the general public find out, there will be panic on the streets. Imagine if we told you there was a deadly spider or killer leopard on the loose?'

'You just have,' chirped Ollie.

'Well, yes, and the Crufts winner has now gone walkies and I'm not sure where it's all going to end. Don't you see, all these animals are *special* in some way? Fastest horse, best dog, deadliest spider, longest snake, oldest elephant. And these are just the ones I know of. There may be dozens more that haven't made the news.'

'And your point?' asked Ben.

'Not a point. A plan. In fact, not even a plan, more of a mission,' said the professor, raising his eyebrow towards Spy Dog. 'The police have been useless. They can't even stop the top dog being stolen from Crufts!'

Lara cleared her throat and glared at him, her doggie pride getting the better of her.

'Er . . . the Crufts winner, not necessarily the *top dog*, but you know what I mean . . .'

Lara nodded. *That's better.*

'So,' announced the professor, breathing deeply and sweeping his hand across the board once again. 'We need to rescue these poor animals. And, great news, kiddie-winks, your favourite world-renowned, award-winning scientist has a cunning plan.'

The kiddie-winks exchanged glances. The world-renowned, award-winning scientist's plans didn't always . . . well – go to plan.

7. The Missing Link

'And action!' yelled Ben from behind the camcorder.

The professor was already sweating. The gorilla suit was heavy and it made every movement difficult. He'd had to remove his spectacles so his vision was very blurred. He sat like he thought a gorilla would sit, shoulders slightly slumped, nose twitching.

'Here is Bob,' announced Ben from behind the camera, 'the world-famous artistic gorilla. He does *gor-ffiti*,' announced Ben. 'Which is like normal graffiti, but done by gorillas. What are you painting today, Bob?'

Ben zoomed in on the professor, marvelling at the realism of the gorilla suit. It was on loan from one of the TV studios that had recently made a series of blockbuster monkey movies.

The professor picked up a paintbrush in his primate hand and dabbed it at the blue pot. Ben wandered round to the canvas side and watched as the gorilla splashed paint on the paper. The professor wasn't very good at art but, as gorillas go, the painting ended up being a rather impressive self-portrait.

Ben panned his camcorder around the room where Bob's other paintings were displayed. 'There's no doubt,' he said, 'that this is the most marvellous monkey on the planet.'

Five minutes later, Ben had set up a Twitter account and was uploading the video to

YouTube. As predicted, Bob's video went viral. Within a day he had gained 200,000 followers and, as the professor had assured him, 'In the modern world, once that happens, the rest will take care of itself.'

Archie never sat. He squatted on the leather chair, while Gus was spreadeagled on the leopard-skin sofa. They had just unloaded a stripeless zebra and a white rhino into their new safari park home and were enjoying some downtime.

'And finally,' said the newsreader, 'how about this for a talented animal?'

Gus slapped his head in frustration. He knew what was coming and that spelt bad news – his night off was cancelled. The footage cut to Ben's YouTube video and then an interview with Professor Cortex, who was still sweating after secretly easing himself out of the gorilla suit. 'I've worked with animals all my life and I'm telling you, Bob is a very talented gorilla,' said the scientist. 'He's the Picasso of the primate world. We've been working with him since he was a baby. He's good at art and music.' The film cut to the gorilla-suited professor clumsily playing some Beethoven. 'We think he's the most talented ape in history and he lives right here at 132 Ambleside Road, Manchester.'

The reporter tucked a strand of hair behind her ear. 'Bob is certainly an amazing find. A Picasso primate indeed. But enough monkey business,' she smiled. 'Back to the studio.'

The news anchor man grinned on the outside, masking his irritation that such a junior reporter could steal his *monkey-business* line. 'Monkey business indeed,' he grimaced, thinking hard about the next link. 'In fact, totally bananas,' he smiled, pleased at his rapid recovery. 'The question is, is it going to be sunny enough to swing through the trees this weekend . . .?'

Archie cut the weather lady off before she'd spoken. The TV went blank just as their boss strode in.

'My night off's cancelled, ain't it, guv,' sighed Gus.

'I want that monkey by first thing tomorrow,' growled the large figure. 'It's what I've been waiting for. It's the missing link.'

8. Bob

Lara and the spy pets watched the news, the dogs' tails wagging in great excitement. Shakespeare was swishing his tail, a little annoyed. *It's not fair that I'm not allowed to go along*, he thought. But he was trying to look on the bright side. *At least I'm part of the mission, even though from the sidelines. It could have been worse – the children have been banished altogether.*

The professor ran through his plan one last time. Shakespeare was new to the spy pets' team but he had already worked out that it was a typical Cortex plan – *slightly bonkers but kind of just about makes sense*. There was a method in the madness.

'We've made the news so it's a guaranteed certainty that the baddies will come after me . . . I mean Bob. Whoever is stealing special

48

animals will surely want our super-special gorilla. So here's the plan and, like all the best plans, it's deadly simple. I'll allow myself, or Bob will allow *himself*, to get gorilla-napped. What the baddies don't know is that I'll be wearing a tracking device inside the suit. GM451 and the pups, all you have to do is follow me and that will lead you to the baddies' hideout. And, bingo, I reckon we'll find all the other captured animals. We simply alert the authorities and, *voilà*, we arrest the baddies and the animals are rescued. Mission accomplished.'

Sounds exciting, wagged Star.

Lara was less enthusiastic. *It seems fairly straightforward*, she thought. *But I have enough experience of the professor's hare-brained schemes to know that things don't always turn out as planned.* She winced as she recalled another seemingly *simple* adventure in a museum and a recent escapade in which Sophie took a death-defying trip in a flying wheelchair. She was pleased that the children had been banished. Ben, as always, had put up a very strong argument but it was a no-brainer. *There is no telling what Mrs Cook would do if the professor accidentally lured her children into another mission.*

It all sounds exciting, thought Shakespeare, *except for my bit!* He swished his tail a little more violently so that the professor would be sure to see his dissatisfaction.

'I've noticed the tail-swishing thing and I understand what you're saying, Agent Cat,' soothed the scientist. 'But I think this is a dog mission. GM451 is an experienced veteran of many missions and the pups are quick across the ground.'

Spud looked down at his paws momentarily, aware that everyone was probably staring at him.

'Well, *quickish*,' corrected the professor, 'and, er, well grounded. Besides, we think there might be water involved,' he continued, looking over at the cat.

Shakespeare stopped swishing immediately. He wasn't too keen on the prospect of taking a dip.

'The dogs have cameras in their collars so everything, the whole mission, is relayed back here to this room, where we need a special agent to monitor the situation; someone with sharp eyesight who won't miss a thing.' Everyone knew that Shakespeare could see perfectly, even at night-time. 'As soon as you find out where the baddies are, you simply send an email to the police and Bob's your uncle. Well, Bob's actually me in disguise, and I'm not your uncle. And I'm not saying you have any gorillas that are actual uncles, but you know what I mean. Your uncle would of course be a cat. I don't actually know who the original Uncle Bob was. I would hazard a guess that it's

a saying from the olden days when *Robert* was a particularly common name. And *Robert*, shortened to *Bob* was so familiar that it became the common vernacular for –'

Lara woofed for quiet, sensing the professor was beginning to ramble, which usually meant he was stressed. 'Paws up if you get the plan?' she barked.

The pups and cat raised their right paws. 'Excellent. Prof, I suggest you get into your hairy suit,' woofed Lara, nosing the furry outfit, 'and we get ready for a little monkey business.'

9. Mission Control

The professor's monkey suit had a tracking device fitted, but Lara and the pups weren't taking any chances. Their aim was to keep him in sight if possible, so the pups were hiding in a bush and Lara was in a flower bed, nose twitching and bullet-holed ear cocked.

Shakespeare was struggling to stay awake. 'It's much less exciting at Mission Control,' he yawned, sipping his espresso and keeping his blurry eyes on the TV monitors. The dogs' collar-cams were streaming live pictures back to base and he also had a radio link to Lara so they could communicate if need be. Shakespeare remembered the professor telling him that a lot of secret-agent work was just a matter of sitting tight, watching and waiting. *I guess this is what he meant*, thought the cat, stretching his tired legs and arching his back.

The professor had taken care to make sure being gorilla-napped was easy, but not so easy as to arouse suspicion.

Gus yanked on the handbrake outside 132 Ambleside Road. All was quiet as was usual at that time of night. The men got out of the wagon and stretched away their fatigue, Gus breaking the silence with a huge release of wind.

'Sssshush,' whispered Archie. 'You'll wake the neighbourhood!'

Gus chortled as he wafted his huge hand across his face. 'I'll poison the neighbourhood,' he choked.

They fixed their night-vision goggles into place and the world went green. Archie reached for his rifle and checked the dart was in place. He was fairly sure he'd only need one but he put the tin of sleeping darts into his jacket pocket just in case. The gates to 132 creaked open and the night-vision glasses picked out a cage in the garden. Gus gave Archie the thumbs up and the men silently crept across the lawn.

The dogs were on full alert, crouched and ready to pounce if things didn't go according to plan.

Back at Mission Control Shakespeare was suddenly wide awake, sitting upright. *We have visitors!*

Professor Cortex had heard the van and *Bob* was pretending to be asleep in the corner of the cage. Inside the disguise the professor's heart was racing, but not for long. Archie was taking no chances. He aimed the rifle at the gorilla and there was an almost silent hiss as the sleeping dart sent the professor's heart from *racing* to *deep sleep*. He slumped to the floor of his cage.

Gus used bolt cutters to sever the padlock and the professor's body was dragged out. Gus put his hands under the gorilla's armpits and did the heavy stuff. The gorilla was dragged across the lawn and secured inside the back of the van.

Shakespeare watched from the safety of Mission Control. While the professor was being drugged and gorilla-napped, Lara and the puppies were busy scampering under the cover of darkness. The spy cat could see that Lara was on top of the van, spread flat, one ear up, gripping the air vent. The pups were in the back, hiding in the straw. The tailgate was lifted and the engine rumbled into life. The spy dogs and the professor were on their way. Shakespeare was excited – this was more like it. He rather liked being in control.

10. The Journey

Shakespeare scanned the various TV monitors, his green eyes flicking deftly from screen to screen. Lara's collar was showing daylight as the van trundled north towards the Scottish border.

The pups' cameras were showing darkness inside the vehicle.

Lara was hanging on, her paws frozen, as they made their way north.

Wherever possible she pointed her collar-cam at the road signs so that Shakespeare could monitor their position.

The spy cat was using a pencil in his mouth to tap out the towns and roads on his iPad. *A right turn off the A6105. Almost in Scotland.*

It was mid morning by the time Lara's camera showed the van pulling up at some huge iron gates. The spy dog dared to peep over the edge and Shakespeare saw *DANGER OF DEATH* signs atop the fence, which was at least six metres high and seemed to stretch for miles. A burly security guard opened the gate and the cat watched as the wagon approached a huge stately home.

Lara tried to press herself flat on top of the roof of the vehicle as the drugged scientist was dragged from the back of the wagon and carried into the house.

Shakespeare then watched some frantic video action as Lara nimbly climbed down

from the roof and collected the pups from inside the van.

That's better, thought the cat as the three video screens lit up.

The dogs sprinted to the safety of some bushes and all three cameras were trained on the stately home.

'Are you receiving, Spy Cat?' woofed Lara quietly.

'Loud and clear,' purred the control puss. 'I have your location. Shall I send the email and alert the authorities?' There was radio silence for a minute. 'I repeat, shall I notify the police?'

'Negative,' woofed Lara. 'Will investigate further.'

Lara and the pups discussed the plan. 'There's no point alerting the police yet,' she explained. 'We've seen the professor being dragged inside but we need more evidence before we call for help.'

'Plus we might be able to solve the whole mystery ourselves,' wagged Star, clearly enjoying the adventure. 'We might not need the police at all.'

Lara nodded. It was probably bending the rules a little but she was excited to be part of the action, and it would be nice for her and the pups to chalk up another victory for dogged determination. Plus, Agent Cat was watching and listening in case there was an emergency.

'So I suggest we enter the building, locate the professor and assess the situation from there.'

'Roger,' woofed Spud. 'I hope he's in the kitchen. My tummy's rumbling. I think we've missed a meal!'

Star raised her eyebrows.

There was a rustling in the trees and Spud thought he saw an iguana. He shook his head and looked again. The leaves were rustling but no reptile.

Must just be the hunger playing tricks on me, he thought before continuing.

Lara was the eldest but still the fastest. She checked that no one was around and sprinted for all she was worth. The blur of black and white sped across the grass towards the next bush.

She stopped, panting hard, before beckoning to Spud and Star. The pups joined their mum.

'Next stop, the front door,' she woofed. Before long, the three dogs were at the huge front door. Lara jumped on to her hind legs and pushed. 'Easy-peasy,' she wagged as the door creaked open.

Star peered in. 'The coast is clear,' she whined. Everything seemed to be going to plan.

Shakespeare was starting to enjoy being in Mission Control. 'The estate is owned by a guy called Lord Large,' explained the mog. 'But I don't think that's his real name.'

The cat had downloaded a plan of the house to his iPad.

'Right turn,' meowed the puss, his fur tingling with excitement. 'The professor's tracking device says he's three rooms away.'

Lara went first, creeping along the wooden corridor, trying to keep as quiet as possible.

'Third door on the left,' instructed Shakespeare, watching the TV screens as live pictures were beamed back to Mission Control.

Lara stopped at the door, her ears pricked and senses alert.

'He's in there,' urged the cat, looking at his tablet. 'The blue dot, the professor, is in that room. From the plans of the building, it looks like it might be an office.'

Lara eyed the pups. 'All clear,' she nodded. There was a tiny pattering of paws as the pups sprinted to join their mum. 'Careful.'

The retired spy dog was enjoying herself.

She nosed the door. 'It's open! So simple!'

She eased through with her nose and there, on the floor, was the professor. He was in his gorilla suit but the head had been removed. He was gagged and tied with his back to them, and seemed very much awake.

11. Triple Crossed

Shakespeare was suddenly beside himself with worry. He'd googled the location, a blue dot showing the dogs were in the middle of nowhere – somewhere on the Scottish–English border. He'd zoomed in. *Huntingdon Hall.* He googled the history . . . and the owner. He downloaded a news report from last year when the new owner took over. *Lord Large?* He'd googled the name. Almost nothing. One brief entry in *Wikipedia.* Shakespeare had done some digging. *It seems the Wikipedia entry about Lord Large has been added by Lord Large himself. There doesn't appear to be any such person, other than the 'Lord Large' that he's invented. Strange*, thought the spy cat. He was gathering information on Post-it notes that were stuck all over the wall. *I've seen them do it in crime dramas on TV.* He added a yellow note that said *Lord Large. No such person?* His green eyes scanned all the clues. *Stolen animals. Special animals. Huntingdon Hall. Electric fence.* There was also a grainy photo of Gus and Archie with the word *animal-nappers* written above. He scratched his head and blinked, hoping the pieces of the jigsaw would eventually fit together.

Shakespeare spun his chair back to the TV screens where the action was unfolding. *Eleven a.m. Looks like the dogs have found the professor.*

Shakespeare held his breath. His green eyes were focused, whiskers twitching nervously. *Something's not right. This is too easy.* All three collar-cams were pointing at the professor and there was panic in his eyes. His head was shaking from side to side and he was desperately slobbering through the socks that had been stuffed into his mouth.

Spy Cat's feline instincts screamed danger. *The van had been waved through the high security gate without being searched. The front door of Huntingdon Hall was open. The office door was open. No guards? It's not right.*

'Abort,' he meowed, staring into the professor's panicked eyes. 'I repeat, abort the mission. And get out of that room!'

Shakespeare almost jumped out of his fur as he heard a massive bang. *Like a slammed door?* All three dogs turned and there was a man. *Three men! With huge guns! They're the kidnappers who took Bob. Plus another man. Lord Large?*

'Spy Dog. We meet again,' snarled Lord Large. 'Remember me?'

Shakespeare averted his eyes as the man dropped his trousers and showed teeth marks on his backside. *There's no need for that*, he thought from behind his paws.

'It's not Large, it's Big,' woofed Lara. 'My arch-enemy, Mr Big!'

Spud and Star were yapping but one of the men had moved towards the professor and pointed a gun at his head. 'Down, doggies,' sneered Mr Big. 'The mad scientist has awoken from the sweetest of dreams into his very worst nightmare.' He laughed, pausing to spit a large black globule of phlegm on to the ground next to the professor.

Spud was sure Mr Big was evil but surely missing two meals would be even more of a nightmare? His tummy rumbled in agreement.

Cortex managed to spit the socks out of his mouth. 'This is quite outrageous!' he began. 'Completely unacceptable. I'm sure we can work things out logically. This evil man has lured you here, GM451. I've heard of some double-crossing in my time but we've been triple-crossed. Possibly even quadrupally so!'

The dogs replaced barking with snarling and Shakespeare strained to hear what was being said. Mr Big kept his gun pointed unwaveringly at the professor. 'Quadruple-crossed,' he purred. 'I like the sound of that. Twice as clever as double-crossed.'

He motioned to Gus, who yanked Spud by the collar, lifting him high. The puppy wriggled and kicked as his oxygen supply was cut short. Lara bared her teeth, her eyes fixed on the men. Shakespeare sat bolt upright as the man produced a sharp knife. He sliced the collar off, the puppy falling to the ground with a yelp. He tossed the collar to his boss. Mr Big looked directly at the camera. Shakespeare could almost see up his nose.

'If you pesky kids are watching this, be warned. If you call the police, the professor and his doggies will be killed. Instantly.' The evil man left a dramatic pause. He smiled, but was deadly serious.

The professor continued jabbering. 'It . . . it was all a trap. He knew I wasn't a real monkey all along. He knew you'd come after me, GM451. He's not after me. He's after you and the pups . . .'

Shakespeare's green eyes grew wide in horror as he absorbed the TV images. A small hairy man started stuffing the socks back into the professor's mouth. 'Tomorrow we're going to be hunted. Help, Agent Cat. Heeeellll–'

And all three TV screens went black.

12. Hunted

Hunted? What does he mean hunted*?* Shakespeare's head was buzzing and adrenaline was rushing through his body. He caught his reflection in the mirror and noticed his fur was on end and his tail swollen. *Ready for a fight!* He remembered his mindfulness classes and breathed deeply. He knew he had to clear his head before any decisions were made. *Stay calm.*

Shakespeare forced himself to have a break. He made a cup of mint tea and enjoyed a sardine. *Oily fish. Brain food. I've been up all night*, he thought, cleaning his whiskers. *And the whole mission now rests on me. I must think like a spy cat to act like a spy cat.*

He spent some more time googling Mr Big, his shoulders sagging as he began to uncover the whole truth. Shakespeare had heard the name whispered but he was a bit like Voldemort — *so scary that his name was rarely spoken*. The cat soaked up information from the professor's case files. *Lara and Mr Big go back a very long way!* The cat slapped *arch-enemy* and *hunted* to the Post-it wall. *Emailing the police is definitely out*. He remembered the gun at the professor's head. *Not good*. The oily fish began working its magic and he ran through some ideas in his feline brain. *Ben*, thought Shakespeare. *He might know what to do*. The spy cat downloaded the dramatic video scenes to a memory stick and bounced out of the cat flap, the beginnings of a plan formulating in his mind.

Ben, Sophie and Ollie just panicked. Shakespeare swiped the iPad on to standby. *That's not doing us any favours*, he thought. *Time to introduce my plan*. The children watched as the cat took a pencil in his mouth and moved to Ben's desk. It was a struggle but he started drawing.

The children peered in. 'He's trying to tell us something,' said Ollie. 'What is it, puss? What are you drawing?'

Shakespeare was frustrated. *It's so hard drawing with a pencil in your mouth. I sooo wish I had hands like you guys.*

'He's so clever,' cooed Sophie, her tummy doing cartwheels of pride.

'Is it a burger?' suggested Ollie.

'A burger?' meowed the puss out of the side of his mouth. *Why would I be drawing a burger? It's a plane!*

'Is it a bird?' guessed Sophie.

A blooming bird? It's a plane. Vroom vroom, a plane! I suppose a bird is a lot closer than a burger. Shakespeare stretched his front legs out to the side to indicate fixed wings that didn't flap.

'Looks like a coat hanger,' suggested Sophie unhelpfully.

The cat spat out the pencil and shook his head. *This is ridiculous.* He nosed the tablet back into action and clicked on the internet. He typed in *drone*, and pictures of spy planes appeared.

'The professor's spy plane?' guessed Ben.

'Get in!' yowled the cat, pointing a paw at the boy. *Electric fences. Can't climb up and can't go over. Can't go under. So I have to fly.* He tore into Sophie's bedroom and searched through the dressing-up box. Two minutes later the puss

73

returned, wearing a fetching Lycra cat suit. *One of the professor's better inventions*, thought the cat. *I've worn it before. It has webbed arms and legs so I can glide from the sky.*

Sophie looked unsure. 'Hang on,' she said, 'so if I've got this right, you want us to fly you in on the professor's plane. And then you're going to swoop down like some sort of superhero cat?'

Shakespeare stood tall and puffed out his chest in pride. The Lycra suit made him feel special. He spread his arms wide, revealing batwings. *I love the sound of superhero*, he thought. *And yes, that's pretty much the plan. This is now a rescue mission. Is it a bird? Is it a plane? No, it's Bat Cat!*

13. The Hunting Party

Shakespeare couldn't think what else to do. Whichever way he looked at it he always arrived at the same conclusion. *If I alert the police the professor will be shot. But if I get the children involved, I will be breaking rule number one.* He decided that getting the children just a little bit involved was the best course of action.

The children were running over the plan one last time. Sophie and Ollie were covering for Ben.

'I'll be gone for the whole of tomorrow, all day and maybe even the night,' he said. 'So I've already acted poorly, moped around, said I've got a headache.'

'And as tomorrow's Saturday we'll say you've stayed in bed. But we keep going into your room and taking you drinks and I can come in and play imaginary computer games,' said Ollie, reminding himself of his role in the plot.

'Yes, because Mum will really worry about me if I'm off computer games. She'll want to take me to hospital or something. So, I'm bad, but not at death's door.'

'And meanwhile,' added his sister, 'we've raided our piggy banks and scrambled a hundred and two pounds –'

'And fourteen pence,' said Ollie, remembering his contribution.

'And fourteen pence,' corrected Sophie. 'Plus Ben has *borrowed* another sixty-three pounds out of Mum's purse.'

'Which is my pocket money, plus some, for the next year. And when Mum finds out that I'm taking part in Shakespeare's mission, I'll probably have no more pocket money, ever! But this is a matter of life or death. We *cannot* tell Mum and Dad otherwise they'll ring the police and that's curtains for our pets. And maybe even the prof.'

Ben knew he didn't have any choice. This was one of those situations where he realized he had to grow up very fast.

Shakespeare was listening intently, collar flashing, taking it all in. *We've all seen the video. This is very serious indeed. The only solution is for me to get inside that electric fence and see what's going on.* He looked again at the wall where he'd scribbled *Rule #1. No danger for the kids.* He drummed his claws on the table. *Ben is part of the plot to get near to Huntingdon Hall, but he will never actually be in proper danger.* Shakespeare wasn't entirely sure he was doing the right thing, but there just didn't seem to be any alternative.

Ben looked around gravely. 'I've booked a taxi for myself and the puss. A hundred and fifty pounds, one way, to the Scottish border. We're taking the professor's spy plane.'

'And my precious puss is risking his life to get inside the baddies' hideout,' said Sophie, cuddling her cat so hard it made his eyes bulge. 'Ben will operate the remote control and my ginger superhero will swoop from on high.'

Shakespeare was purring. He loved being cuddled and he was making the most of it. *But if cats were meant to fly, we'd have feathers!* He was a positive puss, *But you never know*, he thought.

As a cat, I'm supposed to have nine lives. Let's hope this isn't my last one . . .

Meanwhile, the dogs had been muzzled. The professor had his gorilla head rammed back on and Gus had superglued it so it was almost impossible to remove.

'This is intolerable!' protested a muffled voice as Gus was doing the gluing. 'It's very hot in here. I find your behaviour most unacceptable.'

Gus just grunted. 'And I find your whingeing most unacceptable. Just doing as I'm told, monkey man.' He kicked out at Lara, who was growling menacingly.

If I ever get this muzzle off – which I will – my teeth will sink so far into your bottom that you'll not be able to sit down for a month.

The professor and dogs were crowded into a cage and Archie turned the key. 'Quiet!' he ordered. 'Our special guests are due any minute.'

Spud looked around. Their cage was in the corner of a huge drawing room. At the other end was a roaring log fire. There were leather sofas and chairs, thick carpets and a huge window showcasing a magnificent view over the estate. Pictures of animals adorned the walls. Spud noticed that most of the pictures were of hunting scenes.

Men on horseback chasing wild boar. Men with flat caps shooting grouse. A man holding three dead rabbits. Always men and always guns! The puppy saw stuffed animals everywhere. *Birds in jars. A fox. A hare. Even a terrier dog, presumably a much-loved pet from back in the day?* To complete the gruesome message a stag's head dominated one of the walls – *check out those Rudolph-like antlers –* its glassy eyes watching from above. *It seems the owners love animals, especially shooting and stuffing them!* There was a tray of drinks on the table

79

and, Spud sniffed, *some nibbles*. Everything was olde worlde except the thoroughly modern curved TV. The dogs watched the screen as a luxury people carrier with tinted windows pulled up at the front door. Three men and a woman got out and the captives watched as Mr Big shook them warmly by the hand. Sixty seconds later the new arrivals entered the drawing room.

Lara and the pups had no idea what was happening but, as the professor had pointed out, in muffled tones, 'If they're associated with Mr Big, one thing's for sure. They are baddies.' The three dogs growled as fiercely as their muzzles allowed. The gorilla-clad professor struggled to his feet and rattled the bars. He was so hot and bothered that he couldn't speak. He just growled.

'Calm down, you rabble,' smirked Mr Big, evidently enjoying himself.

The visitors made for the champagne and nibbles. There was clinking of glasses as they set about the task of draining the drinks. The lady wandered over to the caged animals, a huge grin lighting up her face. Her eyes lingered a moment upon Lara. The dogs strained at the bars and the professor jumped up and down with rage.

'Well, hello, fellas,' said the lady in a very posh accent. The dogs were muzzled but their eyes said it all. 'Ooooh. So wild!' The woman kept her distance. 'Lord Large,' she shouted, 'are these some of the ones we'll be hunting?'

'Take a seat, Gloria,' oozed Lara's arch-enemy. 'Let me explain what's going to happen. Tonight we celebrate this gathering of some of the wealthiest and best hunters from across the planet. Tomorrow, we test our wits against the best that nature has to offer. It will be the ultimate battle to see who will prevail – man or beast.' Gloria raised an eyebrow. 'Or woman,' Mr Big added hastily. 'Whoever shoots the animals with the highest score will be crowned this year's *crack shot . . .*'

Crackpot, more like, muttered Lara.

'. . . And will, of course, be invited back again next year to defend their title.'

So they get the chance to spend even more money on next year's entry fee, clicked Lara. Mr Big was out to make a killing in more ways than one. He was going to be super-rich if he could find enough animals to hunt every year.

The evil baddie wandered among his guests, handing out the colour-coded darts like a big kid in a poisonous sweet shop.

Making his way over to Gloria he handed over the darts, drooling, 'For you, my dear. My favourite colour – red for dead.'

The assembled group looked around eagerly. Right on cue, the door opened and Gus and Archie wheeled in a trolley laden with weapons. Lara's eyes went from wild with anger to wide with fear.

'As you know, I have assembled the world's finest collection of *special* animals. We have five hundred acres of rolling hills out there. I've taken great care to collect the rarest of breeds. Pandas, for instance.'

One of the men could hardly contain his excitement. 'That, Sir Large, is total genius. I don't think any of us has ever bagged a panda.'

Mr Big nodded, savouring his own evil genius.

'I am keen to give you a new kind of thrill. If you're spending a million pounds to enter, you'll be wanting something special. We have everything: a snow leopard, lion, Grand National and Crufts winners. Special snakes,

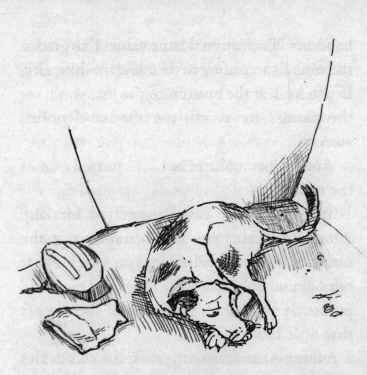

spiders, a cheetah. Several primates. A white rhino. We even have one of the Queen's corgis.' He paused while a 'Wow!' swept through his customers. 'I have royal blood,' he lied, 'and therefore some *special* connections.'

Lara's throat emitted a low growl. *You don't have royal blood. You have evil blood!* Her ears were pricked, listening and learning, desperately trying to figure a way out.

'Here is the score sheet,' explained Mr Big, Archie darting between the hunters with a handout. 'Each animal has a value. I've graded the animals according to their level of difficulty. If you look at the bottom of the list, you'll see the pandas are worth ten thousand points apiece.'

'And points make prizes . . .' purred one of the men.

'But pandas are easy,' suggested Mr Big. 'Sluggish. Rare, yes, but certainly not the ultimate hunting challenge. You will see that our one and only cheetah is a hundred thousand points. It will take a professional shot to get that little beauty.'

A large American man cracked his knuckles and strode over to the weapon trolleys. 'Looks like I'm going to be baggin' myself a li'l ol' fast cat,' he said, picking a rifle and looking through the sights.

One of the other men looked confused. He jabbed the top four names on the list. 'Gorilla, two hundred thousand points. Puppies, three hundred thousand points and "Spy Dog", a million points? What makes these creatures so special?'

Mr Big had been looking forward to this question. He rose from his chair and wandered towards the cage where, predictably, Lara, the pups and the professor jumped to their feet and started to vent their anger. The animals threw themselves at the bars. 'These,' he shouted above the growling, 'are my most prized targets. Some, like the dogs, have sentimental value. The black and white dog is especially tricky. I acquired it from MI5. It's the world's first ever *spy dog*. Trained to kill! And these yapping puppies are not just full of noise. They are a menace to society.'

'You're the menace!' woofed Spud, his muzzle pushing through the bars.

'And the monkey?' asked the lady, seeming particularly interested.

'For a start, Gloria, it's not any old monkey. The gorilla is very talented. One of a kind, hence the big bonus points. Nicknamed *the Picasso Primate*, he can talk and paint. You might have seen him on the TV. I've tamed him, you see. He was completely wild when I captured him.'

The professor had never been so angry. He rattled the bars of his cage and his muffled voice rang out. 'Wild? I was livid! Grrrr. Let me out of here right now . . .'

The lady looked startled. 'He really does talk! And he sounds very angry indeed.'

The American had swapped his weapon. He pointed a pistol at the gorilla and did an imaginary shot. 'BANG!' he said. 'I'm excited, Your Lordship. You've got my juices flowing. Spy dogs and talking gorillas. A million of your British pounds is a bargain. Tomorrow, I'm having your critters at the top of my list.'

The shooting party trailed out of the room, eagerly anticipating the following day's sport. Gloria paused for a moment in the doorway and looked over towards the dogs. Lara sensed she wasn't quite as eager as the others.

Mr Big smiled to himself as he led the guests to the drawing room. His plan was working perfectly. What the guests didn't know was that the darts they were using were tranquillizers; the animals would appear to be dead but would wake up in a week's time. By then the hunters would be long gone, and the creatures would be thrown in a cage until next year. No one would ever guess – one elephant looks like any other, after all. *It's recycling, really*, he chuckled, *shooting the animals again and again.*

14. Fight or Flight?

Ben met the taxi at the end of his road. The driver loaded his suitcase and his sister's old doll's pram into the boot and the boy jumped into the back, with his rucksack.

'Just you?' asked the driver, looking at Ben in the rear-view mirror.

'Just me,' he grinned, trying not to show too many nerves and casting a glance backwards, half expecting Mum to be rushing down the road shaking her fist. 'Meeting my family up north,' he said unconvincingly. 'My mum said to give you this,' he added, wafting £150 in the driver's face. That seemed to do the trick.

The car started and they were away. The boy was in the back seat, the spy plane was in the boot and the cat in the bag.

★

Mum was looking hassled. 'But why can't I come in?' she asked, attempting to peer past Sophie into Ben's room.

'Because he's just said he doesn't want any visitors,' lied Sophie. 'He's got a sore throat and a funny tummy and guess what, Ollie's been playing computer games and worn him out.'

'So he's sleeping,' shouted Ollie from inside the room. 'He says he doesn't want any tea either.'

'If he's off his food, maybe he needs to go to the doctor's?' Mum shouted. 'Benjamin, are you all right?'

Ollie did his best low-pitched grunt, trying to sound like a twelve-year-old. Luckily for the children the phone rang and Mum was caught in two minds. 'Well, tell him I'll be coming to see him after he's had a snooze,' she said, running down the stairs. 'With a thermometer.' Mum wasn't at all convinced, but thought she'd play along for the time being.

'Phew, that was close,' said Sophie. 'I hate lying to Mum.'

'It's not really lying,' explained Ollie. 'This is a mission. Sometimes agents have to do

what's right. Not what their mums think is right. I mean, you never hear James Bond's mum saying, "No, James, you can't go and save the world because you need an early night." '

That settled it. They drew the curtains in Ben's room and plumped up the pillows so they looked, as far as possible, like a sleeping boy. Sophie was worried. 'I hope our *real* brother is making some headway.'

It was 10 a.m. Ben, his suitcase, pram and rucksack had been dropped off in a small village that his iPhone said was three miles from Huntingdon Hall. The taxi driver had left after demanding a 'tip', and the boy immediately felt isolated. He had no money and no food. He pulled his hoody tight and zipped it up. Scotland was chilly. He unzipped his rucksack and felt a little better as Shakespeare peeped out, his eyes blinking in the daylight, his translating collar blinking in anticipation. There was no time to lose. Shakespeare led the way, Ben struggling with the luggage until they were on a straight bit of road away from prying eyes.

The spy cat struggled into his Lycra suit while Ben set about assembling the miniature plane. 'I hope there are no cars,' he said as he placed the plane in the middle of the road. 'That's west,' he continued, looking at his

Google Maps app once more. 'So Huntingdon Hall is two miles as the crow flies.'

Except it won't be a crow, thought the cat, holding his front paws aloft and checking his underarm flaps were in place.

Ben positioned the old doll's pram behind the plane and tied the two with a piece of rope. 'I've tied it to the handle of the pram,' explained the boy. 'But when you lift off, the pram will hang downwards. You'll be dangling,' he said, holding up the pram at the handle end to demonstrate. 'And swinging. You need to be holding on very tight.'

Shakespeare's translating collar blinked, taking it all in.

'Quickly, puss,' he hissed, 'I can hear a car.'

The Lycra-suited cat jumped into the pram and took a deep breath. He held his paw aloft – *Go, go, go* – and Ben stood back. He pressed his thumb on the *start* button of the remote control and the small engine spluttered into action. Ben had never flown a remote-controlled aeroplane, but he was hoping his knowledge of computer games would help. He noticed the red roof of a van coming round the corner. 'Here we go, puss,' he yelled. 'Ready for take-off!'

The boy pushed the lever forward and the plane started to taxi, following the white line of the road. The post van had rounded the corner and was coming straight at them. Ben pushed the lever further forward and the plane accelerated, the pram trundling behind.

They picked up speed, the pram bouncing dangerously on the tarmac. Shakespeare's ears were flat, his eyes watering. The van was getting closer. *We need lift-off. Quickly, Benjamin!*

Ben wasn't sure how to make the plane take off. He tried to remember what the professor had said. 'When it reaches a certain speed the engine will cut out and wind-power takes over'? *Or something like that* . . . Ben pushed his thumb against the accelerator stick. The small engine squealed and the boy could hardly watch as the plane sped towards a collision.

The post lady had been doing this round for twenty-three years. The weather was variable but the routine was always the same. This was the only straight piece of road. She always used it as an opportunity to multitask – scanning the letters while shuffling her playlist . . .

She had sorted the letters for the next village and noted that Jamie McCullough had six

items. *Must be his birthday*, she smiled. She glanced up and saw a small aeroplane and a pram careering towards the van. The lady shielded her eyes and slammed on the brakes just as the aeroplane rose into the air, the pram dangling below. She couldn't be sure but there seemed to be a cat waving at her. And was it wearing a red suit?

The back wheels of the pram skidded across the windscreen and made a clattering noise on the roof of the van. She swerved. The van hit a ditch, the lady's seat belt jarring her to her senses. The airbag knocked her backwards and she sat for a few seconds, not quite believing what she'd seen.

The post lady released her seat belt and heaved the van door open. She fought the airbag and staggered out of the van into knee-deep cold water. The lady crawled up the side of the ditch and on to the tarmac. She looked up and down the straight bit of road. *Nothing*. And into the sky. *Nothing*. Apart from a nosebleed she was fine. But at that moment she decided twenty-three years was long enough. Jamie McCullough would be her last delivery.

15. Crash Landing

Shakespeare was terrified. His pram was swinging erratically in the wind and he kept looking up at the rope, hoping Ben had tied a good knot. *The boy was right about dangling*, thought the cat, cocooned in the hood of the pram, his claws fully extended and digging in as he dared to peer below.

He'd watched the countryside floating by and then, *Hey presto, a stately home and some very high fences.* Shakespeare looked for a place to make a safe landing. Memories of a previous adventure raced through his mind. He had used the cat suit before. *And nearly died!* He remembered what the professor had said. 'It doesn't allow you to fly but it will enable you to glide.' He had then shown a wildlife video

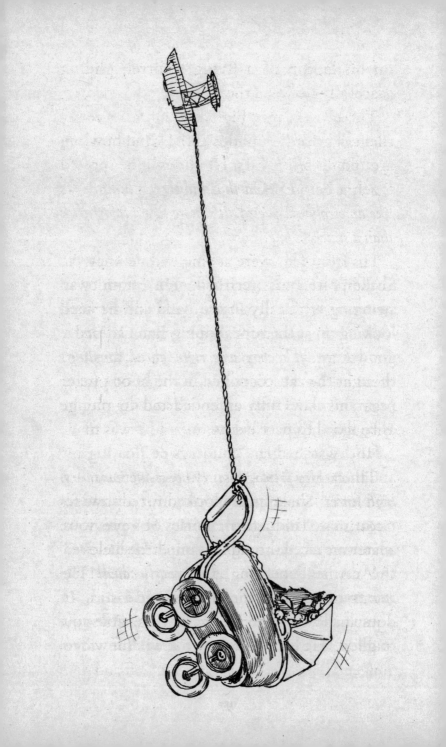

on his laptop of a flying squirrel, gliding gracefully between the trees.

The cat was very high and the plane eerily silent. The only sound was the wind howling around his feline ears. He thought he spotted a zebra below. *And that large grey lump looks like an elephant! Weird. It's more like a safari park than a stately home.*

His front legs were aching and he knew he couldn't hold on much longer. He decided to go for it. With a deep breath and a determined yowl Shakespeare retracted his claws. *Whoosh* – he was away. The plane continued its silent journey. Shakespeare was a tangle of ginger legs and red Lycra as he started to plunge through the air. He sure hoped he was made of the right stuff.

The cat was falling fast. His legs were tangled and his tail vibrated as he plummeted towards Scottish soil like a furry comet. His eyes were watering but he could see some trees below.

'And they're coming at me very *faaaaast*!' He remembered the squirrel video and instead of squirming, he extended his legs. All of a sudden, his descent slowed. The spy cat was no longer falling. *I'm gliding!* He leant left and then right, swooping, looking for a place to land. He meowed at a pigeon, almost scaring it to death.

He glided over a lake, his white belly skimming the water, before landing in a heap and rolling over in the grass. The cat picked himself up. His right paw was limp and he spat out a tooth. *Apart from that, not a bad landing.* Shakespeare had gone from Mission Control to missing in action. He decided to do what trained secret agents do best and headed for the nearest tree to do some spying.

The flying cat was long gone. He looked around and suddenly felt very alone. A chill wind seemed to spring up. Shoving his hands deep into his pockets he took one last look at the horizon before setting off back down the road. It would be a long walk home.

16. Hunters Gather

Lara, the pups and the gorilla-clad professor had been released into the grounds. *I've been in some scrapes*, she thought, *but this has to be my most dangerous mission. There's nothing stately about this home.* The spy dog led them to some dense bushes where the small group crouched, panting. The professor was already struggling. 'You go without me,' he pleaded dramatically. 'I'll only slow you down.'

'Professor Bob here is our priority,' woofed Lara to the pups. 'He's trained us to be spy dogs. We owe him. We need to keep our wits about us at all times,' she added, thinking aloud. 'There are wild animals out here.'

'And even wilder hunters, with us at the top of their list,' shivered Star.

'So we work as a team and survive for as long as we can,' reassured Lara. 'How about we turn the tables? Instead of waiting around to be *hunted*, we become the *hunters*.' Spud's tummy rumbled loudly in agreement.

'Do you think help will be coming, Ma?' woofed Star. 'Do you think Agent Cat might have called the police?'

Lara shook her head. 'Unlikely,' she woofed gently. 'Mr Big warned us that would mean certain death. We cannot rely on Spy Cat to rescue us. Look, kids, I don't want to sound unkind, but this is a serious mission and Shakespeare's just a cat.'

Gloria and the men had breakfasted. The overnight stay had given them an opportunity to get to know each other a bit better and suss out the competition. Everyone wanted to win and prove they were the *crack shot*.

The American had double-breakfasted. 'You never knows where your next bellyful's comin' from,' he drawled while loosening the belt on his camouflage trousers.

He assessed his three competitors. Finishing a croissant was an Arab sheik. *Probably a spoilt*

rich boy who knows next to nothing about this kind of warfare. Desert boy. Camel shooter. The other man, furiously tapping at a laptop, was a British banker who had more money than sense and who was seeking an adventure that got him out of the office for a few days. *From desk job to dead job*, the American mused. *Unlikely.* And 'Glorious Gloria'. *All designer labels and no substance — glamorous and stupidly rich but couldn't hunt her way out of her designer handbag.*

Then again, he thought, *you have to be stupidly rich to be invited to this particular safari*. He was sure he would win. He'd been brought up in a country where it was OK to own a gun. He had been using rifles before he could walk. The American didn't feel fully dressed without a gun in his hand – only then was he trigger-happy. He looked again at the score sheet. *The pandas don't seem worth it. Those critters are too darn slow and those white patches make easy moving targets. I'd love to bag that chatty li'l chimpanzee. I wonder what his last words will be? And, for a cool one million poochy points, that MI5 spy dog is my number-one target*, he thought to himself. The American knew there could only be one winner and he fully intended it to be him – whatever the price.

Archie, Gus and Mr Big made a dramatic entrance. Each hunter had chosen their weapon and were armed with four darts, each set a different colour to distinguish who had bagged what.

'It's a competition,' reminded Mr Big. 'See who can shoot the highest points score by nightfall. At the end of the day, we will collect the . . . er . . . dead animals and assess the colours. One of you hunters will be crowned this year's *crack shot* and lift this magnificent trophy.' Mr Big gestured to Gus, who lifted a slightly dented tin jug. Gus grinned, but it didn't make the prize look any more impressive.

Mr Big hastily walked across the entrance hall and swung open the massive oak door of Huntingdon Hall. The hunters filed out, every one of them keen to bag something extra special.

'Let the hunt begin!'

17. Double Bogey

It was midday. Shakespeare nosed his way to the top of the tallest tree on the estate. He peered towards the hall and scanned the gardens. *Nothing.* He turned and looked east towards Huntingdon Hall's very own golf course. *A panda, lying spreadeagled, with blue ink all over it.* Somewhere in the back of his mind he knew you could get an eagle in golf. *But a panda?* He shimmied down the tree and scampered towards the bear. Shakespeare remembered his first-aid training and checked the pulse. *Still alive. In fact, breathing very deeply.* The cat scanned the panda for signs of injury. *Nothing. It's rather odd but I think this giant panda is asleep!*

A golf buggy approached from the trees and Shakespeare legged it to the edge of the

pond, crouching low, whiskers twitching. He recognized Gus and Archie from last night's video nasty. The puss peeped as they hauled the sleeping panda on to the back of the cart. As Archie managed a three-point turn, Shakespeare sprinted out of the bushes and jumped on to the trailer. *Take me to your leader!*

Mum had been suspicious all morning. Ben hadn't showed at breakfast time and his brother and sister were acting strangely. She had decided to give them the benefit of the doubt and let the children carry on with their game.

That was this morning. This afternoon Mum had decided it was time to open Ben's bedroom curtains. It was fair to say that she didn't like what she saw.

One hour later Mum had reached a state of numbness that was way beyond anger. Dad had telephoned the police and Sophie and Ollie sat in the lounge, sobbing, while the police lady asked awkward questions.

'I went in to draw the curtains and his body was just a bunch of cushions and pillows,' said Mum, still not quite believing what she was saying. Sophie and Ollie seemed just as upset as Mum. They'd tried to do the right thing and got it very wrong.

'So you have no idea where your brother actually went?' asked the police lady. She was specially trained to keep calm.

Sophie shook her head and snivelled. 'I can't remember.'

'He's gone a hundred and fifty pounds away,' wailed Ollie.

'And where on earth did he get a hundred and fifty pounds from?' gasped Mum, who seemed specially trained to explode.

Ollie's eyes darted, just for a millisecond, to Mum's purse. 'You have got to be joking!' she erupted.

The professor had been deposited in a garage. 'It's the safest place,' Lara explained to the pups. 'He's a liability. Remember, not only are there four hunters out there, but there is also a whole herd of wild and dangerous animals.'

Star gulped. 'Lions?'

'And a cheetah, remember,' woofed Spud, sucking in his belly and wondering how fast his little legs could actually go.

Lara and the pups decided their best course of action was to be hunters rather than wait to be hunted. They figured that at least that way they could see what was coming. They left the professor and, noses to the ground, ventured out into the arena. They did some animal spotting. 'It's like a really wild game of bingo,' wagged Star. 'Zebras, an elephant, a racehorse.' Lara hoped their number wasn't up.

'I saw a crocodile in the lake,' Spud reminded them. 'And a tarantula in that bush.'

The animals approached the perimeter fence. Lara looked at the warning sign. She picked up a stick and threw it at the fence. There was a fizzle and a crack, the stick turning to instant charcoal.

'No escape that way,' she woofed. 'Let's keep exploring.'

It wasn't long before Lara's powerful nose caught a scent. 'In fact,' she sniffed, 'two scents. Two of the hunters are close by. Keep low. Here's the plan . . .'

The Arab sheik and the banker were both stalking the one-million-pound dog. Lara

made sure of that. She was walking deliberately slowly, making herself as big a target as possible. She was shaking with fear. *I know there are two hunters lining me up in their sights. Timing is everything.*

Spud was watching the sheik, who was creeping in from the east.

Star was watching the banker crouching in the bushes to the west of Lara.

Little did they know it, but a rather large lion stood some distance away, watching them all. Lara was right – timing was going to be crucial. Both men settled into firing position, their sights fixed on the top prize. Spud waved his paw towards his mum. *Left a bit*, he signalled. The target moved and so the men shifted

position. Each knew they would only get one shot at the million-pound mutt and were keen to make it count. When they were perfectly lined up Star barked the signal and Lara sank to the ground. The men fired a fraction later, more in panic than accuracy. Both stood. The sheik had shot the banker and the banker the sheik. Both men looked at one another aghast, then at the darts embedded in their legs. And then they fell.

Lara punched her paw in the air. 'Sweet dreams!' she woofed.

'Two down,' signalled Spud. 'One man and one lady to go.'

The lion decided to move in and take a closer look.

18. Stuffed!

Shakespeare jumped off the back of the buggy as soon as it became clear what was happening. He scrambled on to a nearby branch, watching and listening as the vehicle pulled up on the lawn and the panda was unloaded. It was placed in a row of exotic animals – *all dead or sleeping* – and all dotted with coloured darts. Shakespeare grimaced; it wasn't a pretty sight.

The men disappeared into Huntingdon Hall and Shakespeare seized his chance. He sprinted over to the animals and checked out his theory.

Two pandas. A racehorse. A cheetah, white rhino and a very long snake. All asleep. There was no sign of Lara, the pups or Professor Cortex. *Maybe they're inside?* Spy Cat's green eyes scanned the house. *I have to get to the bottom of this. And my gut feeling is that I'll find the answers in there.*

It was Spud's sensitive nose that first sniffed out the American. 'Over there, in the long grass,' he said, jabbing his paw wildly. 'Yellow darts.'

'I'm the fastest so I'll handle this part,' wagged Star.

The puppy circled the American, slinking low until the time was right. Then with a quick yap she was away, bounding towards the edge of the lake. Star didn't need to look round to know the man was in pursuit, the ground vibrating with every step as he lumbered after the dog.

To the man's amazement, the puppy jumped into a boat, started the motor and sailed off towards the island in the middle of the lake. He'd heard of walkies – *but dinghies*? A yellow dart thudded into the side of the boat, causing Star to duck while doing her best to keep the craft pointing in the direction of the island.

The American consulted his price list again. 'No wonder you're worth three hundred thousand points, little critter,' he said. 'You sure is special.'

Another boat was handily moored nearby, so the man reloaded his rifle and jumped aboard. The chase was on.

Star's boat thudded into the island and the pup leapt ashore. Another yellow dart hissed into a tree. *Too close for comfort!*

By now the pursuer had jumped out of his boat and was wading ashore. 'Here, boy,' he coaxed. 'Come on, li'l friend.'

'I'm a girl,' growled Star, attempting to encourage the man a little further on to the island, 'and most certainly not your friend!' She lay low in the long grass at the base of a tree as he staggered on to dry land. Star froze, sensing she wasn't alone. Ever so slowly she turned her head to look directly into the eyes of a cheetah. The cheetah looked scared. Star smiled reassuringly. 'You'll be OK. Just stay still,' she whispered.

There was a click. The American's gun was cocked and ready to fire. Star took a stick in her mouth and waited. She heard footsteps squelching closer. *Just a little longer.* As he walked past her hiding place the puppy jerked her head and the stick sailed through the air. The man aimed and shot, his dart hitting the stick. *Good shot*, thought the puppy as she darted in the opposite direction, back towards the boats. She didn't dare look back. *I assume he's reloading; that'll give me the few seconds I need.*

The puppy bounced into the dingy, pulled the cord with her teeth and the engine spluttered into life. She tried to keep her head down as the boat slowly chugged away from the shore. Star opened her mouth and grabbed the rope attached to the other boat as she sailed by, towing it with her. Another yellow dart whizzed past her ear and hissed into the water.

She dared to look back. The man was jumping up and down with rage, realizing he'd been marooned.

'Come back here, stupid dawg!' he yelled. He started wading into the water but retreated fast as one of the crocodiles showed itself.

Star couldn't help a silly doggie smirk spreading across her face. *He's probably low on ammo. He's trapped on an island that is guarded by crocs – not to mention that cheetah. It's certainly not me that's stupid.* She raised her ears in

triumph. *I'd say this part of the mission has been a huge success!*

Shakespeare dug his claws into the ivy and climbed up the wall of Huntingdon Hall. He'd removed his Lycra suit, not wanting to attract unnecessary attention, hiding it in a flowerpot in case he needed it again later. The puss crept in through one of the upstairs windows and dropped silently to the floor. He slinked his way out on to a very long carpeted landing. The spy cat cocked his head and listened. *Faint voices. Downstairs.* He padded silently down the winding staircase, back arched, ready to fight or flee.

Shakespeare's whiskers twitched and he darted behind a suit of armour, sensing someone was coming.

After a moment, Gloria tentatively poked her head out of a side room and looked both ways before quietly scurrying towards the front door and slipping out. *Strange*, mused the cat. *But then again it's hardly surprising that baddies are up to no good.*

The cat reached the last stair and looked around at the vast trophy room. The stag's head dominated the wall above the fireplace, with a rack of guns in a cabinet to the side. *And stuffed animals everywhere!*

He silently jumped up on to one of the huge tables to take a closer look. *A badger, perfectly animated. A fox, growling, its sharp teeth preserved for evermore. Stuffing animals? It's a weird thing for humans to do, but they sure do it well.*

Shakespeare was startled as he heard a door slam and footsteps clip down the corridor. He glanced around. *The door is opening and there is nowhere to hide!*

Mr Big, Gus and Archie burst into the room. Shakespeare tried to stay calm. He recalled his spy training: *A good agent thinks on his paws and blends into the background.* Shakespeare stood still, one paw raised, with what he hoped was a neutral look on his face. *Blending in*, he thought, *means I have to look like a stuffed animal. It's a high-risk strategy but hiding right under their noses is my only chance!*

Shakespeare's ears were cocked. His eyes were fixed straight ahead but he was straining to watch out of the corners. *One thing is for sure. Mr Big is very angry.*

The evil man clicked a remote at the huge TV screen. 'Three guys down,' he cursed to Archie and Gus. 'Two of the idiots seem to have shot each other. And Ronnie is stranded on the island. Look at the idiot. He's had to climb a tree to escape the croc!'

The statuesque cat stifled a laugh. *Sounds like Lara and the pups are doing OK.*

'Gloria is out there somewhere but I don't fancy her chances. Those dratted dogs are working as a team. And her being such a girl and all that.'

Lara won't like that comment! Go, spy dogs! thought Shakespeare, daring to blink.

'And that gibbering ape is on the loose too,' Gus reminded them. 'So what's the plan, Boss?' he asked, thumping his fist into his other hand. 'Shall I do what I do best?'

'Eventually,' smiled Lara's arch-enemy, calming down a little. 'But first of all I'll do what *I* do best. I'll devise a deadly plan.'

Shakespeare's body stayed rigid but he dared to move his eyes. Gus was wandering towards the table. *Yikes!* The cat's expression froze and he tried to stand especially still, one paw raised, staring into the distance. *Spy Cat needs to look stuffed.*

Shakespeare could smell that Mr Big had lit a cigar. Gus was standing right next to the table. *He's examining the stuffed animals! Stay away, you idiot. Otherwise you'll be the next to get stuffed!*

Gus had picked up the preserved raven next to Shakespeare. He gazed closely and ruffled its black feathers.

'So what's the deadly plan, Boss?' he said, replacing the bird and turning his attention to the ginger cat. 'This puss is *amaaaazing*,' he cooed, moving so close that Shakespeare could smell his kebab breath. 'So lifelike!'

The cat's eyes were achingly dry and he was desperate to blink. His heart was thumping but he didn't dare breathe.

'The plan is this,' snapped Mr Big, removing the dart from his gun. Gus turned his attention to the plan and the statuesque mog snatched a breath and blinked. He moved his head slightly to get a view of the men.

'As you know, we issued the hunters with sleeping darts. So although they think they've taken out these exotic animals, they've actually

put them to sleep,' explained the baddie. 'At the end of the safari the hunters move on, the animals wake up and we throw them into a cage to use again next year. Of course one or two of them might not actually wake up, but so what? We've got plenty – we can afford to lose a few.'

'We love that, Boss. Double-crossing at its best. You sure is evil,' slathered the big buffoon.

Mr Big inhaled deeply, the end of his cigar glowing with pleasure. He loved compliments. He puffed the smoke into Gus's face. Shakespeare shuddered as Mr Big took a tin from his jacket pocket and inserted a new dart.

A black one . . .

'Special darts for the blithering monkey and our dog squad,' he said, shaking the tin.

'Special?' asked Gus.

'Deadly poison,' smirked Mr Big. 'It's time for the monkey to be silenced once and for all, and for Spy Dog to finally DIE, DOG!'

19. Closing In

The police had contacted all the taxi firms in the area and, sure enough, A2B taxis had taken a booking to drive a boy 150 miles north. The driver was questioned and the final destination discovered. The Scottish police had been alerted and things were moving swiftly.

The Cooks were being given a very fast police escort. Mum was crouched behind the wheel of the people carrier with a look of steely determination. Dad and the silent children were on their way north. It was a stormy afternoon and the windscreen wipers worked a double shift as the car sped towards the Scottish border. It was darkening. Mum's face matched the weather.

★

Mr Big had explained that if a job needs doing it needs doing now. The weather had closed in as Mr Big, Gus and Archie strode out into the night. They were dressed in bright yellow heavy-duty weatherproof hats and coats, and each had a powerful torch. Mr Big had a rifle but the others couldn't be trusted. Archie had a baseball bat and Gus his fists. The rain lashed down and lightning occasionally illuminated the sky.

Lara had been very firm when hiding Professor Cortex in the garage. She'd held her paw up in front of his face – 'STAY,' she'd woofed. 'We're going to catch the baddies. You just stay hidden.'

She couldn't have been clearer but the professor hated staying put. He'd used a screwdriver to remove his superglued gorilla head and was wandering around in the rain when the torch lit him up.

'Is that you, GM451?' he asked, squinting into the light.

The professor complained very loudly as his arm was shoved up his back. 'That jolly well hurts,' he said. 'And this gorilla suit is wet and heavy. Look here, Big, I know we've had our differences over the years but I'm sure there's some good in you somewhere. Let's go back to your office and work this whole thing out. I'm appealing to your nicer side.'

Mr Big laughed so loudly that his smoker's cough revved up. Rain ran down his face as he spat something black and gooey at the ground.

'This side is evil,' he snarled, pointing to his left side. 'And this side is even more evil. There is no niceness and you, monkey man, are bait. Gus, hold him.'

Gus took over, the professor crying out in pain as his arm was yanked even higher up his furry back.

'Spy Dog!' bellowed Mr Big, shining his torch into the darkness. 'We have the professor. Show yourself or it's curtains for Cortex!'

Shakespeare knew he'd only get one shot. He perched himself on the windowsill and remembered the paintballing exercise. Mr Big had walked three metres from the professor. Archie was with him, with Gus taking up the rear. The beams of their torches were reaching into the darkness, illuminating a torrent of raindrops.

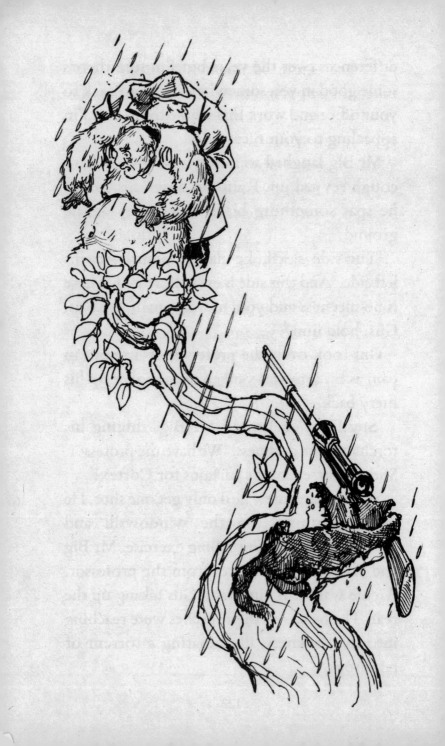

The cat squinted through the sights. He'd taken the opportunity to grab one of the rifles from the trophy room and was struggling to get to grips with it.

The trick is to miss the professor and shoot Gus! Keep still, chaps, thought the cat.

Shakespeare waited for the right moment, his fur soaked through to his bony body. *I hate rain!* He eased his paw on the trigger and the red dart hissed from the rifle. Gus fell to the floor with a splash, the rain beating against his body. The professor looked around.

Run, old man, run! urged the cat, and the professor did exactly that, half man, half gorilla disappearing into the blackness.

20. A Shocker!

Mr Big looked from the rapidly disappearing professor to the prostrate body of Gus and back again. He was keen to hunt Lara down but nothing was more important to him than saving his own skin. Someone was firing at him! He decided to cut his losses.

Archie was driving the golf buggy and Big was in the passenger seat, black-darted rifle pointing ahead. The rain was still slashing down. Lara saw the headlights heading for the exit. *No way, we can't let him escape!* Adrenaline pumped through her body and she left the pups trailing. It was a long and windy road and she'd calculated that she could cut the buggy off if she went cross-country. Lara arrived just ahead of the vehicle, standing tall, blocking the road. The buggy sped round the corner on two wheels. The headlights caught sight of Lara's white patches and swerved, skidding into a ditch and causing Archie to hit his head. Mr Big cursed as he disentangled himself from the wreckage. Torch in one hand and rifle in the other, he turned to face the spy dog.

Shakespeare was soaked to his skin. He was tired and hungry but neither was an excuse to slow down. *This is a mission! And I'm in the middle of it!* He chased the buggy and watched it career off the road. 'Noooo!' he yowled as he saw Lara caught in the torchlight. Mr Big was pointing the rifle at his beloved spy dog. *A black dart. No way!*

Shakespeare's body ached with tiredness but he kept running. Lara growled and edged forward.

Mr Big growled and stepped back. 'Poison dart, poochie!' he yelled into the rain. 'Especially for you.'

Lara bared her teeth and growled, unsure what to do. *I'm a spy dog and I'm quick. But not as quick as a poison dart!* Her thinking was cut short by the rifle shot. The black-tipped dart embedded itself in Lara's chest. She leapt at the man, in one final effort, determined to leave her mark. His torch fell to the ground and Mr Big screamed as Lara sank her teeth into his leg.

And then it went quiet.

After a pause the man stood and rolled the lifeless dog away with his foot.

'Heel.'

Shakespeare yowled as he watched Lara fall.

Mr Big looked to the heavens, rain lashing into his eyes. He howled at the clouds, victorious, as lightning ripped the sky. He was the *crack shot*! The sound of whirring rotor blades signalled the celebrations would have to wait, however.

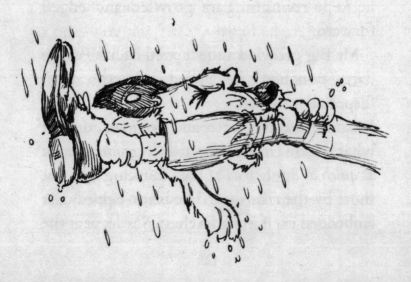

Mr Big turned and ran like a wounded animal. He knew the fence was near. He was a clever man. He knew that if he could escape he could set up another evil empire somewhere far away. With the dog gone, everything would be a lot easier from now on. So the police helicopter was a bit of a downer. Big's torch was gone so he stumbled blindly through the darkness, Shakespeare tracking him. The police searchlight swept over them. Shakespeare waved but the light kept moving. Mr Big stopped to catch his breath. He stood under a tree, trying to escape from the downpour and the prying light of the helicopter. Shakespeare extended his claws and bounded up the tree.

Big was weighing up his options when, all of a sudden, he heard a terrifying yowl and a furry Fury fell from the heavens. Shakespeare had just enough energy to hang on to the man's face, wrapping his legs round the back of his head like a ginger octo*puss*. The man couldn't breathe. He tore wildly at the cat, pulling at lumps of ginger fur, but Shakespeare held on, his claws sinking into the skin behind the baddie's ears. After a few seconds of struggle

Mr Big managed to pull the cat away and threw him to the ground. Shakespeare was winded but he righted himself, arched his back and hissed at the man. He swished his tail, his white teeth gleaming in the rain.

'You've killed my beloved Lara,' hissed the puss.

'A cat?' smiled the man, dabbing the scratches behind his ears and looking a little relieved and somewhat amused. 'A bedraggled, flea-ridden moggie,' he laughed, the noise drowned out by a clap of thunder.

'Not any old cat,' hissed Shakespeare. 'A spy cat. Trained by the best, on missions to catch the worst. And you, Big, are the lowest of the low.'

Shakespeare weighed up the situation. *The man has no gun, but he's picked up a baseball bat.* There was a brief spark as the electric fence lit up. *So we're near the perimeter.* The cat noticed that the helicopter searchlight was coming back his way. *My best course of action is to keep the baddie here until the searchlight falls on him.*

The cat hissed again. The helicopter came closer, the trees blowing wildly under its rotor blades. Mr Big stepped back, baseball bat swinging. The noise was confusing. The fence buzzed again as the rain hammered down. The cat stepped forward, tail swishing and every piece of fur standing on end.

'You've killed Lara!'

'You're just a cat!' yelled Mr Big, remembering the professor's shouting from yesterday about a 'spy cat'.

Shakespeare saw doubt in his eyes and took strength. The rain was coming down even harder now.

'I am not *just a cat*!' he yowled into the darkness.

Shakespeare was overcome with grief. He was cold, wet and scared. He let it all out in the biggest caterwaul of anger he'd ever managed.

Mr Big looked terrified. He stepped back and the fence buzzed. The helicopter blades were chopping the air and it was raining confusion.

Shakespeare let out another yowl, this time a big cat roar. The helicopter's light illuminated the man as he stepped back too far. *DANGER OF DEATH!* Shakespeare shielded his eyes with his paw. The evil man was in for a nasty shock.

Electricity, rain and baddies don't mix.

21. A Cat's Life

'You were amazing,' said Sophie, stroking Shakespeare's ginger fur and trying to avoid the bald patches. 'I mean, you didn't know there was a lion behind you when you had him trapped.'

I did think I'd done a rather large roar, smiled the family cat. *I guess it proves you don't have to be a big cat to have a big cat roar! I have to say, it's the most amazing mission I've ever been involved in and it was most certainly a team effort.*

Mum just tutted. She'd been in the police helicopter and had seen the final showdown. The doctor had given her some pills that had helped calm her nerves afterwards, and now she sat in the chair, rocking gently, not really with it.

Lara was also a bit groggy, her eyelids at half mast. 'And for once, the pups and I were just minor players. This, Agent Cat, was very much your mission. We put you in charge of Mission Control and you ended up taking control!'

'A team effort,' he reminded them. 'And Gloria helped,' admitted the puss, purring with delight as Sophie tickled the top of his head.

'What's happened to the hunters?' asked Sophie.

Professor Cortex was looking pleased – not only to be out of the gorilla suit but also at the capture of the villains. He eyed Mum nervously, dreading what would happen when she came off the pills. 'All's well that ends well,' he said, daring to sound perky. 'That horrible American man is behind bars. Well, he will be as soon as he gets out of the hospital. That croc sure took some chunks out of his ankles. He and the sheik and the banker are all charged with "hunting endangered species". I mean, you can't just go around shooting pandas and suchlike.'

'And Gloria?' asked Ben. 'If I understand it right, she was a goodie?'

'Posing as a baddie,' nodded Professor Cortex. 'As we now know, Gloria is an undercover reporter for the *New York Post*. She posed as a wealthy heiress to gain an invite to Big's evil safari. She was a great help. Gloria was working on the inside, gathering evidence. She's got herself quite a story!'

'And she rescued me,' Ben reminded the prof. 'She was going for help. Picked me up from the side of the road in that terrible storm.' He sneezed to demonstrate the point.

'Gloria's into animal rights,' smiled Sophie. 'I mean, aren't we all?' she said, squeezing her beloved ginger cat so hard that his green eyes bulged.

Yes, and this animal's got the right to be squeezed slightly less tightly, he thought.

'She's a very clever lady,' noted the professor. 'And extremely brave. She noticed the thefts, tracked them to Huntingdon Hall and then took a huge risk posing as one of the hunters. If it wasn't for Gloria switching Mr Big's darts, GM451 would be more than a little sleepy.'

'She made sure those black darts were actually only sleeping darts. Otherwise Lara would never have woken up,' shuddered Ben, patting his pet.

The professor's chest was swelling with pride. 'Gus and Archie are locked up, awaiting trial on all sorts of charges. The list of offences is as long as your arm. And, let me tell you, Archie has very long arms. All the animals have been safely returned to their homes – and some of them showed some genuine spy potential, I must say!'

The children chuckled, wondering how an undercover elephant might fit in.

'And the mastermind himself?' asked Ben. 'Lara's arch-enemy? Lord Large, or rather, Mr Big?'

'Well, it seems he's going to be all right. Third-degree burns to his back and legs so he's pretty well bandaged from head to foot.'

'That leccy fence must have been a bit of a shock,' beamed Ollie, not realizing how perfect his words were. 'I bet he's in lots of pain,' he added, a little too enthusiastically.

'Oh, plenty of pain,' smiled the professor, also a little too enthusiastically.

Lara and the pups couldn't resist wagging.

Good job Mr Big's behind bars, purred Shakespeare. The cat cast his gleaming green eyes around the lounge. *Mum wasn't in the best of shape but, rule number one, the children are safe and well. My beloved Lara is sleepy but alive. The pups are wagging. And best of all, I'm being stroked by the most wonderful girl in the world.* He purred loudly as his mind ran through the adventure. *I started with a coordinating role and ended in a life-saving role. I jumped from a pram dangling from a*

plane. I wore a special superhero suit. I shot Gus and I helped capture Big. He hoped he'd done enough to be included in the next mission.

The puss sank deeper into Sophie's lap. *Once my bald bits have grown back, that is.* Shakespeare lolloped on to his side and raised his paws just enough so Sophie could access his white underbelly. He closed his eyes in sheer bliss. *It's great being a spy cat. But even better being a family pet.*

'Mr Big is of course denying everything,' smiled the professor. 'But you can never deny the truth.'

22. Lie Detector

High-security police cell, Scotland Yard, London

Mr Big was bandaged from head to toe. Bumping into the electric fence was the equivalent of being struck by lightning. He'd developed a twitch. He wore dark glasses to protect his puffy eyes and a baseball cap to protect his sensitive scalp.

'It's all a big mistake,' he said. 'You can't prove anything. I was just doing a simple gardener's job at Huntingdon Hall.'

'And you knew nothing at all of an illegal safari scam?' asked one of the detectives.

Mr Big twitched as he tried to look horrified. 'That's such a terrible accusation, Sergeant,' he said, adjusting the professor's newly invented thinking cap. 'I'm offended.

Are you calling me a criminal? I have feelings, you know.'

The police officer in the next room purred with delight as he watched the laptop screen. *Of course I knew about it. It was my idea! I was going to finally get rid of that dratted dog and get rich in the process. And those pesky interfering pups.*

'And you know nothing of the plot to kidnap pandas from Edinburgh Zoo?' enquired the police officer.

'Nothing, Officer, I swear,' came the words from his mouth.

I planned the whole thing. And Red Drum. And the Crufts winner, came the words on the laptop. *I am the most evil genius in the world. Too clever for you. The police will never ever get me to admit anything . . .*

Six months later . . .

Mr Big looked rather small, standing alone in his prison cell. He squinted through the iron bars and watched the rain beating down. Some might say he looked like a caged animal.

He turned and sat down on the single bunk and stared at the bare brick wall. It wouldn't

be long before he was out of there. He hadn't yet worked out how to escape, but he knew he would find a way – he always did. And, when he did, he knew exactly where he was heading. The hunt wasn't over yet – in fact it had only just begun . . .

From safari to skyscraper . . .! Turn the page
for a sneak peek at another exciting

adventure . . .

1. Ken's Invention

Fifty-five years, three months and two days ago . . .

Even by old-fashioned standards, Mr Dewitt was old-fashioned. He'd risen to head teacher by insisting things were done the right way. *His* way. It was a very simple system. He would write on the blackboard, in exaggerated loopy handwriting, and the children would copy it down. Facts mostly. And if it wasn't done properly then it had to be done all over again. 'Dewitt Again' made sure of that.

6D smelt of egg. In the winter the smell of egg was overpowering. In the summer the stench was even worse. Mr Dewitt ate egg-and-cress sandwiches for his elevenses, egg-and-cress sandwiches for his dinner and egg-and-cress sandwiches if he needed a snack in-between

times. It would be fair to say that Mr Dewitt liked egg. He also had a plentiful supply. Every morning for the past fifty years, the headmaster had wandered down to the chicken shed at the bottom of his garden, returning shortly afterwards with half a dozen freshly laid eggs. Every single day. Mr Dewitt knew a thing or two about chickens. In fact, he considered himself to be a bit of an 'egg-spert'.

In his classes there were very few questions and absolutely no nonsense. If they weren't copying things from the board, the general rule was that the children worked in silence. And if they were copying things from the board, the general rule was that the children worked in silence too. Silence ruled while he wandered between the pupils, shoes creaking, occasionally walloping his ruler on to the desk if a child appeared to be slacking.

Which is why he loved his two top students, Maximus and Kenneth. No ruler was required. In a lifetime of teaching, he had never known ten-year-olds with such keen minds; brain-boxes that soaked up information. For him, Maximus and Kenneth were proof that copying from the board was the way forward. After all, if it worked for them, then it should work for everyone. Even better, the boys seemed to spur each other on, both trying to be top of the class. They excelled across the board – if you discounted sport, that is; they preferred to exercise their brains instead. Maximus was slightly chubby and insisted on keeping his white lab coat on, even in PE. He'd recently received a football in the face and his spectacles were held together with a sticking plaster provided by matron. Kenneth, on the other hand, was tall and gangly. Although he looked built for long-distance running, he often struggled to coordinate his limbs and found himself spreadeagled on the track. He was a running joke.

But what the boys lacked in PE, they made up for in mathematics and science. And here they were, about to demonstrate their skills at the esteemed end-of-year head-to-head 'show-and-tell'. Mr Dewitt believed in competition. He'd drummed it into the children that taking part was for wimps. It was the winning that mattered. Kenneth and Maximus had spent the entire Year 5 working on their own top-secret science project that they were about to demonstrate to the class.

A slightly nervous Kenneth was up first. 'Ah-hem,' he began, clearing his throat. There followed a long pause. Everything about Kenneth was long. His long, slender fingers led to overgrown, yellowing fingernails that tapped impatiently on everything he touched. A slightly crooked nose seemed to protrude from the middle of his pimpled forehead and continue down to a thin, pointy chin. Even his own mother probably wouldn't have considered him a 'looker', even if she had really bad eyesight. His nostrils flared with every breath, accompanied by a high-pitched whistling as the air was sucked all the way up. A steady stream of snot continually oozed out; only to be licked from his top lip by a long, lizard-like tongue.

'Thank you, sir, for allowing me to address the class,' he blurted at last.

Mr Dewitt nodded. 'Get on with it, laddie,' he said. 'It's sports day, so we all want to be outside.' In other words, Mr Dewitt wanted to be outside.

'Err . . . Yes, sir. As you can see, I have written a few ideas on the board behind me.'

Forty children gasped at the series of diagrams and equations that filled the entire blackboard. All looked completely bemused, except young Maximus, who sat nodding appreciatively. *Chemical imbalances in the barometric pressure of the atmosphere. Impressive.* He knew the bar was set high.

'I have been investigating the atmosphere,'

announced Kenneth. He turned to an object on Mr Dewitt's desk and whipped off the tea towel, revealing a small metal dish with an antenna. 'This is my Climacta-sphere 1960.' Mr Dewitt's left eye twitched: he didn't like surprises. Unless he had agreed to them first, of course.

Kenneth was encouraged to hear someone stifle a 'Golly gosh'. He continued with renewed confidence.

'The Climacta-sphere 1960 shoots particles

into the sky.' He paused for effect, eyes darting around the room. 'And I have found a secret ingredient that has the power to change the weather.'

There was an audible 'Wow!' among Kenneth's classmates. The headmaster twitched again. Emily's hand shot up. Mr Dewitt trusted Emily to ask a good question, so he nodded approvingly.

'Wowee! So you can create sunshine!' she beamed. 'You can make it so we don't have dreary grey days?'

There was a pause as Kenneth's feet shifted awkwardly and he looked away. 'My experiments are in the early stages,' he mumbled through his nose. 'At the moment, I can create the opposite. As you know, my father owns a chicken farm and I've harnessed the power of chicken waste to create clouds.' He extended a bony finger, pointing at the left-hand side of the board. 'This is how it works.'

His audience looked on, goggle-eyed at the jigsaw of chalked numbers and letters. 'Small scale at the moment,' he admitted with a shrug. 'You might have noticed, I've managed to create a cloud at home?'

Forty pairs of eyes grew wider still as they tried to picture the eerie farm on the hill above the town. It sure was dark and thundery up there. Come to think of it, the farm was almost always hidden behind a cloud these days. Emily's hand shot up once more. She got the nod. 'I don't get it,' she said. 'What's the point of dark, grey clouds when you could have nice blue sky?'

Kenneth Soop's mouth opened but no words came out. He was devastated. Emily – wonderful Emily, the light of his life, the girl he admired from afar – didn't get it. What's more, she was putting the boot into his invention. *Emily didn't like it* . . . His droopy shoulders slumped and his long nose pointed to the floor as he heard the other children mumbling in agreement. Kenneth was only ten years old but he already knew he was different. He loved darkness and clouds. He'd recently experimented with adding more of his secret formula and his hilltop farm had enjoyed thunder and lightning for a whole week. He'd sat in his bedroom gazing through the storm at the sunny town below and had never felt happier. He just didn't understand why everyone else seemed to like gloriously hot, sunny days. For Kenneth, grey was the new blue.

'A jolly good effort,' congratulated Mr Dewitt, not sounding particularly jolly. 'A secret ingredient that changes the weather is, indeed, of considerable scientific importance. Maybe just needs a little refinement before it's ready to go,' he barked, with a twitch.

Young Kenneth tried not to sag on the outside but part of him was shrivelling on the inside. His classmates didn't get it. Mr Dewitt didn't get it. He blinked back hot tears and the urge to run and hide. One day, he vowed, everyone would realize just how valuable a dark cloud could be.

'Next up,' prompted the head teacher, nodding to the ten-year-old in a white lab coat, 'young Maximus Cortex.'

DISCOVER EVEN MORE ABOUT
THE SPY PETS...

SNIFFING OUT DANGER WHEREVER THEY GO!

Meet them at their OFFICIAL WEBSITE

spydog451.co.uk

IT'S PACKED WITH:

- Top-secret extracts
- Grrrreat gossip
- Cool competitions
- YOUR ideas
- Andrew's school visits and events
- Fun pictures and videos

PLUS

- Chat and blog with Andy, Lara,
Spud and Star, and Shakespeare
- Enter the monthly
Talented Pets competition

AND MUCH, MUCH MORE!